The Puppy Predicament

Rachel Anderson

Late November

THE PUPPY PREDICAMENT

BY RACHEL ANDERSON

Published by Late November Literary

Winston Salem, NC 27107

ISBN (Print): 978-1-7341008-6-0

ISBN (E-Book): 978-1-7341008-7-7

Copyright 2020 by Rachel Anderson

Cover design by Sweet N' Spicy Designs

Interior design by Late November Literary

Available in print or online. Visit latenovemberliterary.com

Library of Congress Cataloging-in-Publication data

Anderson, Rachel.

The Puppy Predicament / Rachel Anderson 1st ed.

Printed in the Unites States of America

Dedicated to

Craig, Lindsay and Tanya for helping keep my dream alive. And to Queenie, Falon, Coco and Roxie . . . the dogs in my life.

***

This book honors
Veterans of the Vietnam War...

Thank you for your sacrifice.

CHAPTER 1

Grandpa's News

Kids clambered onto the bus, pushing and shoving and making a lot of noise, but Emily Hanover ignored them.

She was too busy staring at a picture of some adorable Beagle puppies. It was Mrs. Green's fault. The school librarian had handed Emily the newest Highlights magazine. "Make sure you bring it back on Monday," Mrs. Green had said.

Emily usually read all the stories in the magazine first. But this time the puppies caught her attention. She ran her hand over the picture and imagined what it would be like to hold one of them.

It wasn't until she heard some arguing that she looked up.

It was the mean Trenton sisters. She sighed. Trouble was headed her way.

"Let me in," Sissy said as she tossed her books toward Emily. "You're hogging the seat."

Emily slid to the window but kept her back to them, hoping they would get the message and leave her alone. But as the bus lurched forward Carol leaned into Sissy who leaned into Emily. Laughing, they squashed her tight against the bus wall. Emily wiggled a bit to gain some room. She could barely breathe.

"Move over," she said through clenched teeth.

"Don't tell me what to do, freckled shrimp," Carol said, "or you'll be sorry."

The school bus bumped along a stretch of dirt road. Four more stops, Emily thought. Then they'll be off the bus and she can have the seat to herself. She opened the magazine and tried to concentrate on the puppy picture. It didn't take long before she began dreaming about having a puppy for herself.

"What are you looking at?" Sissy demanded.

Emily hugged the magazine to her chest. "Nothing."

"I saw the picture. Let me have it."

Emily clutched the magazine tighter. "Leave me alone."

Sissy reached over to snatch it, but Emily pressed the magazine against her shirt.

Finally, Sissy began talking with other students which ended the torment. Emily stared out the window, counting the telephone poles as the bus passed them. When she saw the tops of the grain silos of the Barnett farm, she relaxed a little. One more stop and the sisters would get off the bus, and she would have peace and quiet.

The bus slowed and then braked to a stop. Sissy tried one more time to get the magazine. Luckily, Emily had kept a good grip on it.

"Come on, Sissy," Carol said. "Let the freckled shrimp dream of puppies. Everyone knows that it'll never happen." Then Carol leaned over and whispered to Emily, "Too bad you couldn't take care of the dog you had." And then, at last, they left.

Emily opened the magazine again, but this time the puppy picture made her sad. What Carol said was true. She didn't have a dog and might not ever have one again. Not now. Not since Queenie died.

Closing her eyes, she remembered the day when she rode her bike down the driveway and Queenie went into the road. Emily had yelled for her to come back, but Queenie was old and couldn't hear well. And then the car hit her and didn't even stop.

Her parents said the accident wasn't her fault, but Emily didn't believe them. Her brother had asked her to take care of Queenie while he served in Vietnam. She'd promised she would. And now Queenie was dead, and Greg didn't even know because Mom and Dad didn't want him to read it in a letter.

The bus braked and screeched to a dusty stop at her house. Emily grabbed her books and shuffled up the aisle. She tapped her bus driver on the shoulder.

"Mr. Allen? Could I have a different assigned seat?"

"Don't let those girls bother you," he replied. "I see how they're acting. If they keep it up, I'm going to talk to their parents."

Oh no, she thought. If Mr. Allen told on the sisters, they'd find ways to get even. "That's okay. You don't have to do that. I'll try to ignore them."

"All right, then. Have a good weekend, and I'll see you on Monday," he said.

Emily jumped off the last step and walked to the mailbox. It was empty. She headed down the long driveway toward her

4

house, still angry at the sisters.

The door slammed behind her as she entered the mudroom off the kitchen. She dropped her schoolbooks and the magazine on a chair and kicked off her shoes. Grabbing a pencil and piece of paper from the phone nook in the kitchen, Emily plopped down at the table and wrote hastily: *Sissy is a brat. Carol is a double brat. I hope they get the chicken pox. Double chicken pox.*

She stared at the words. The bullying had started in May, just as school ended, and she had no idea why. Sometimes the older girls, like Carol, acted like they were better than everyone else. Sissy was in 6th grade, same as Emily, but not in the same class *thank goodness!* Secretly, Emily hoped the sisters would move to another city. Better yet, to another state, maybe even another planet.

She drew stick figures on the paper and added monster faces. She named them Sissy and Carol. That made her feel a little better.

"Is that you, Emily?" Mom's voice carried from the basement.

"Yes," she responded.

"I'll be up in a minute."

As she studied her drawings, the screen door squeaked loudly and Grandpa Hanover came into the kitchen.

"Hey, there's my girl. How was school today?"

Emily crumpled the paper. Not even Grandpa could cheer her up right now, especially with Carol's mean words still echoing in her ears. "Okay, I guess."

"Just okay?"

Emily nodded.

Grandpa sat next to her. "I have a surprise for you that might make this a great day."

"Really?" She perked up a bit.

"Yep, and it has something to do with puppies."

"Puppies?" Emily jumped up, tossing aside her grumpiness. "What puppies?"

"Well," Grandpa said. "I heard about them a few days ago."

"Heard about what?" said Emily's father. He stood outside at the kitchen screened door. His arms and face were streaked with grease and dirt. "Is it something to do with the boys?"

Emily stiffened. Whenever Dad mentioned "the boys" he

6

meant Greg, and their neighbor's son, Paul, who were both in in the Vietnam War.

"No, son. It's something else," Grandpa responded.

"Emily. Get me a glass of water, would you?" Dad asked.

"Sure." Emily grabbed a glass from the cupboard and ran the faucet until the water was clear and cold. "What's wrong with Dad's truck?" she asked Grandpa.

"Something with the engine," he answered. "He's been working on it since noon."

That's not good, Emily thought. Her dad wouldn't be able to deliver appliances to hardware stores in nearby cities. He called the truck their bread and butter, and would say, "No truck, no bread and butter."

"Are you going to tell me about the puppies," Emily asked.

Grandpa winked. "In a minute or two."

She took the water outside to her father. He guzzled most of it, poured the rest over his head and used his handkerchief to mop his neck. "Hotter than Frannie's grill on a busy day," he said.

"Come inside and cool off. Grandpa has something to tell us."

"Will do. I'm ready for a break." He got to his feet, stepped out of his dirty overalls which covered his everyday clothes, and together they entered the kitchen.

Mom came up from the basement carrying a basket of laundry for the clothesline.

"Oh, hello Henry," she said to Grandpa. "What are you up to today?"

"I came by with a bit of news for everyone."

Emily poured a glass of milk and took it to the table along with a plate of peanut butter cookies. She sat beside Grandpa and nibbled on a cookie as Mom brought over a pitcher of iced tea.

Grandpa cleared his throat. "I've been checking on Winston Brock lately. I'm worried about him being all alone. His broken leg hasn't healed right."

"I've stopped by with food, but he won't take it," Mom said. "I don't know what more I can do."

Dad leaned back in his chair. "Winston's stubborn. He won't accept charity."

Grandpa nodded. "He seems to like it when I stop by, though. Now, my news is about his prize hunting dog, Lilyanne. She had a litter of pups a month ago."

"She did?" Emily squealed. "Can we go see them right now?"

"Hold on," Grandpa said. "Winston forgot to latch the barn door one night. Lilyanne got loose and took her pups with her. She's been hiding them ever since."

"Why would she do that?" Emily's heart began to thump.

"Momma dogs often move their pups around to keep them safe," Grandpa replied. "Now, the pups are mutts. Unfortunately, Winston doesn't give a hoot about mutts. Purebred hunters, like his retrievers, are valuable. He takes pride in them."

Emily knew what a mutt was. It meant the father dog wasn't a purebred Golden Retriever like Lilyanne. "What's he going to do with the puppies?"

"That's what I'm going to find out," Grandpa answered. "With Paul gone, he'll have his hands full taking care of the place, his dogs, and those pups."

"I recall that Dandy Lady had a litter of mutt pups last year," Dad said.

Emily grabbed his arm. "I heard Mr. Brock killed those puppies. He didn't even try to find homes for them. We have to protect Lilyanne's puppies."

"Now, calm down," Dad said. "That was a rumor and it proved to be false. Winston took them up to Gladwin, to a relative."

Emily slid back in her chair. The kids at school had said Mr. Brock killed the puppies, but nobody knew why. Her mind whirled. She didn't know what to believe.

Mom drummed her fingers on the table. "Seems to me Winston should have taken better care of Lilyanne and Dandy Lady. He should have kept them safe from stray dogs seeing how they are his prize hunters."

"I agree, but mistakes happen." Grandpa rubbed his chin. "Here's the point to my story. Winston's been putting out food and water for Lilyanne, and she's eating during the night. Most likely, she has her pups close by. They'll be all right so long as their momma's eating. I'd like to get one of the pups for Emily. It'll make a great family dog."

Silence filled the kitchen. Emily peered at her parents over her glass of milk. She was sure they were thinking about Queenie, which would make them think about Greg.

Finally, Dad spoke. "We don't need a dog right now."

"Dogs are good for the soul. It's time you had another one," Grandpa said. "Look, the pups aren't weaned yet, won't be for another week or two. Think it over." He rose from his chair and winked at Emily.

She gave him a weak smile. Grandpa had tried his best, but she'd have to convince her parents she could take care of a dog.

"See you all tomorrow," Grandpa said as he left.

Emily put her elbows on the table and rested her chin in her hands. "Can we get a puppy? Please?"

"Dogs require a lot of attention," Dad said. "Who would train it? I'm not home as much with this new truck route."

"I'll train it, Daddy. I'll be with it all the time."

"That's easy to say, honey, but dogs are a lot of work," Mom added. "I'm sorry, but I agree with your father. Maybe we can get a dog later."

"I can't let anything happen to the puppies," Emily said. "They could be killed, and you don't care!"

"We do care," Mom said.

"But they're not our responsibility," Dad added. "Mr. Brock will do right by them and we need to keep out of his business."

Emily pushed away from the table and ran to the door.

"Come back here," Mom called.

Emily didn't listen. She flew down the steps and through the yard. She ran past the tool shed, the garden, and the old oak tree with the tire swing at the edge of the farm. She finally collapsed beneath an apple tree in the orchard.

Numbness swept through her body. She rolled onto her back and stared at the branches full of ripe apples. It's not fair, she thought. They'll never let me have a dog. Not now, not ever, never!

She closed her eyes and breathed deeply. She wondered what the puppies looked like. Lilyanne was a beautiful retriever with golden, blonde hair. Her pups would be cute; cute and warm and cuddly. Since they were mutts, they could be any color, even different colors. Still, they'd be cute, she was sure.

Emily sat up. She wanted to see the puppies and hold them.

But first she had to find them.

CHAPTER 2

The Search

Emily ran through the dry, stubbled hay field that stretched between their farm and Mr. Brock's. Grasshoppers popped around her and tiny moths flew in her face. She batted them away. With each step she grew more determined to find those puppies.

She stopped at the edge of the driveway and scanned the yard. Mr. Brock's truck wasn't there. Good, she thought. She'd find the pups and would be the only one to know their hideaway.

Emily searched the yard and bushes around the farmhouse. She peered under the wide front porch. She walked through the garden. She even looked inside the small sheds at the edge of the yard. No Lilyanne. No puppies.

"Lilyanne," she called as she headed toward the big barn. "Where are you?"

Suddenly, the air exploded with barking. Emily ran toward the noise.

Behind the big barn, inside the long, rectangular kennel, Mr. Brock's hunting dogs barked in chorus. Sir Taylor and Dandy Lady ran back and forth inside the kennel while Knight, the oldest, sat watching. He panted heavily in the heat of the late afternoon.

"Shhh, don't bark," Emily said when she reached them. The dogs jumped against the chicken wire, tails wagging. They poked their noses into the fence, begging for attention. Emily stuck her fingers through the wire to calm them down. Even Knight came to the fence.

She knew these dogs well. She'd visited them often while tagging along with her brother when he came to see Paul. Queenie used to come along, too. Emily swallowed hard and leaned against the kennel.

"Do you know where Lilyanne and her pups are?"

Sir Taylor barked once and licked her hand.

Emily felt sorry for them cooped up all the time. She wanted to let them out, but Grandpa had said these dogs weren't pets. They were specially trained for hunting. Emily couldn't remember the last time she'd seen them out of their kennel. When Paul was home, he had exercised the dogs all the time. Sometimes, he walked them all the way over to her house.

If she had a dog it would never be penned up all day and night. Her dog would have lots of room to run about. She'd play with it every day.

Her dog? Yeah, right. It would take a miracle.

Knight and Dandy Lady stared at her, tongues lolling, and she noticed their water bowls were empty. Emily ran to the pump near the garden. She raised and lowered the handle several times to prime it. When the water finally gushed out, Emily took the pail that hung on the pump and filled it half full. As she made her way back to the dog pen the cold water slopped over the sides of the pail and into her shoes, but that didn't stop her.

Inside the pen, she moved the water bowls near the fence where she could fill them from outside. The dogs drank every drop of water, ambled over to the shaded part of the pen and stretched on the ground. Emily refilled their bowls. After that, she carefully looked around the pen and frowned. It was filthy. She would tell Grandpa. He would make sure the kennel got cleaned.

Emily continued her search for the puppies. She came upon two empty bowls near a dirt road that led to the woods. Her heart soared. Grandpa was right. Mr. Brock was feeding Lilyanne! The puppies would be growing bigger and stronger every day.

Oh, she needed to find the pups. See them. Hold them!

She hurried down the road looking for signs of them.

"Lilyanne?" she called. "Where are you, girl?"

At a bend in the road, where it turned to go to the flats by the river, she came to an old two-story shed. Some of the side boards were rotting away and the roof had a hole in it. Thinking the pups could be inside, Emily slowly opened the creaky door and stuck her head in. Sunlight streamed through the hole in the roof making dust particles sparkle. The air inside was hot and dry. Everything smelled musty like damp wood and stale grain. Barrels were stacked in the corners while tools and tractor parts covered the floor. Cobwebs hung everywhere. Spooky.

"Lilyanne? Are you in here?"

Screech, screech, scratch.

Emily's heart pounded up into her throat. She froze. What was that? She pulled back into the sunlight, rubbing the goosebumps on her arms.

Screech, scratch.

Looking up, she saw it was just a branch scratching against the roof. Her breath whooshed out in relief. But then another noise made her turn back to the door. She cocked her head and listened carefully. It sounded like a whimper. Emily leaned inside and she heard it again.

Timidly, she stepped into the shed. "Lilyanne?"

She heard the whimpering sound and clapped her hands together. "Come here, girl. Come to Emily."

As the cries grew louder, Lilyanne appeared. Emily sucked in her breath at the sight of her, all skinny and hair matted.

"Hi there. I've been looking all over for you."

Lilyanne woofed softly, turned and disappeared into the clutter.

Emily picked her way through the shed. Cobwebs brushed her face and clung to her sweaty skin. She prayed there were no spiders. Spiders gave her the creeps. But she wanted to see those puppies so bad even spiders wouldn't stop her.

She found her way to the stairway that led to the second floor. A sliver of daylight cut through the broken boards and gave a bit of light to the small space beneath the stairs.

Puppies! Emily grinned at the sight of them. They were adorable.

She knelt and stroked Lilyanne's neck. Then she touched one of the pups. When Lilyanne didn't growl, or show any concern, Emily picked up a sandy colored pup and cradled it in her arms. The pup stiffened and cried out, which made the others whimper.

"Don't cry, little one. I won't hurt you."

The pup shivered and yelped, louder and louder until Emily put it down. Lilyanne licked her baby several times and it quieted.

Emily sat back and wrapped her arms around her knees. She counted nine puppies. One was caramel-colored, one had flecks of gold, and another one was reddish brown. A few of the pups were solid in color, while others were a mix of colors. Six puppies had long hair, and three had short hair.

And then, one more pup wiggled out from beneath Lilyanne. Number ten. It had short hair the color of a ripe pumpkin. It was such a little thing, much smaller than the others. She held it belly up – a girl. The pup whined and shivered until Emily held it close. She smelled like sweet, warm milk.

"You're little, like me." She rubbed her cheek against the pup's soft hair. "Some of the kids on the bus call me names like teeny or short stuff because I'm smaller than other sixth-graders. And I have freckles. See?" She held the pup's face to hers. "Don't worry, Pumpkin. I'll take care of you."

Emily heard the faint ringing of the dinner bell. "I have to go," she said, putting Pumpkin by her mother. "But I'll be back soon."

Jumping to her feet, she looked at the pups one last time. After dinner, the rescue would begin.

CHAPTER 3

The Rescue

Emily sprinted for home. She had to be in the house before the bell rang a second time. Dinner time was dinner time. No ifs, ands, or buts.

By the time she reached her farm, she'd come up with a rescue plan. She ducked into the garage. A few minutes later she found her old wagon and pulled it across the dirt floor. The wheels squeaked a little and wobbled a lot, but it still rolled okay.

Next, she found a cardboard box big enough to hold the puppies. It was dusty and a bit dented, but once she straightened the box it stood a little higher than her waist. She set it on top of the wagon and pulled the handle. The box toppled off. Emily put it back on and gave the wagon a tug. It fell off again. She groaned. There must be a way to make it stay in place. How else would she carry ten puppies at one time?

Dad entered the garage. "Where have you been? I've been looking for you."

Emily gulped. "Um, in the orchard and down by the flats."

"Did you hear the dinner bell?"

"Yes."

Dad took out his pocket watch and tapped it. "Better get a move on."

"Okay," Emily replied. "Are you eating with us?"

He shook his head. "I'm taking the truck to Joe's garage. Hopefully, he can fix it yet tonight." He looked behind her. "What's the wagon for?"

"Collecting rocks." The lie popped from Emily's mouth.

"Rocks? What kind of rocks?"

"Big ones," she said, adding another lie to the first.

"I see. Well, don't keep your mother waiting."

Emily left the wagon in the garage and hurried to the house. She felt terrible for lying and was a little surprised Dad

21

hadn't noticed. It must be because he's worried about the truck, she thought.

"Sorry I'm late," Emily said as she rushed into the kitchen.

Mom turned from the stove. "You've been gone for two hours. Where were you?"

"Out behind the orchard," Emily said.

"Look at me," Mom said.

Emily looked.

"You worried me running off like that."

Emily gave her a big hug. "I'm sorry."

"Are you okay?" Mom asked.

"Yes," Emily said.

"Hmm, if you say so." Mom raised her eyebrows. "But after dinner we're going to discuss those puppies."

Emily filled her plate from the stove, sat at the table and gobbled down the mashed potatoes, peas and chicken. Mom talked about this and that, but Emily wasn't listening. Her thoughts were filled with puppies. She had to rescue them tonight.

Mom's chit chat was interrupted by four short rings of the

party line. The phone call was for them.

"Clara speaking," she said as she picked up the phone. "What? Oh sure, honey. I'll be right there."

"What's wrong?" Emily asked when she hung up.

"Your father needs a ride home. Mr. Jones can't work on the truck until morning."

"Will Dad lose another day of work?"

"Possibly, but it can't be helped. Let's go pick him up."

"Can I stay here?" Emily asked. "I'll clean up the kitchen."

Mom gathered her purse and keys. "Well, I suppose. But don't go wandering off again. We'll make a stop at the grocery store and should be back in an hour."

After Mom left, Emily hurriedly washed and dried the dishes. She covered the leftover food, put it in the refrigerator, and wiped down the counter and table. After that, she dashed to the garage. *It's puppy rescue time!*

Carrying the box, she dragged the wagon through the farmyard and down the path that wound through the woods at the edge of the Tebewee River. The trail had been worn smooth from years of flooding and from cows going to and from pasture. She'd taken this path many times with Greg when he went to see Paul. Nowadays, she was the only one who used it.

She set the box on the wagon and pulled it along without a problem until the wagon hit a big bump and the box fell off.

Emily studied the box. How could she get it to stay in place? Greg would know what to do. He had great ideas. Whenever Emily got stuck on a problem, her brother would say, "Do something. Anything." Emily would, and it usually worked. She walked around the wagon and rocks came to mind. She'd told her dad she was collecting them. Rocks might work.

In a matter of minutes, she'd found six good sized ones. She placed the box back on the wagon, tilted it a little, and dropped the rocks inside one at a time. Emily pulled the wagon a few feet, and the box stayed put. Box problem solved.

But it was harder to pull the wagon with the extra weight inside. By the time she reached Mr. Brock's farm and the spooky shed, she felt dizzy. She wiped her sweaty face with the bottom of her shirt and stepped inside.

"Lilyanne? I'm back." No sounds greeted her. No cries, no whimpers. Emily made her way to the stairway. When she looked beneath the stairs her stomach clenched and her heart sank. The pups were gone.

24

Where could they be? She hadn't been gone long. Maybe an hour, or had it been two hours? Her hands turned clammy as a sudden, sick feeling swept over her. Mr. Brock might have come home and found them. Maybe he took them away.

Emily left the shed and ran up the lane. She passed by the barking dogs, rounded the big barn and stopped. The driveway was empty. She leaned against the barn, gulping air, and realized Lilyanne must have moved the pups again.

She plodded back to the shed. Lilyanne sure seemed determined to keep her pups hidden, Emily thought. If she didn't find them soon, she'd have to scrap the rescue plan for tonight. She had to be home before Mom and Dad returned.

Staring down the lane, thinking of where the pups might be, Emily saw Lilyanne cross the road and enter the tall grass next to the old cow pasture. Emily sprinted after her. She found where the grass had been parted and followed the trail to a small clearing. Lilyanne lay next to a hollow log, panting heavily, while the pups played in and around it.

"Poor mommy," Emily said. She bent down and stroked the dog's neck. "I want to help you, girl. We'll move your pups one last time, but this time I'll do all the work."

Emily returned to the wagon and pulled it over to the tall grass. She dumped the rocks out of the box and went to fetch the puppies. She caught the rust colored pup first and carried it to the box. Lilyanne followed close behind her, and the rest of the pups followed their mother.

That was easy, Emily thought. One by one she put the pups in the box, and right away they yipped and yelped and scratched to get out.

"You'll be fine," Emily told them. "Soon you'll be safe with lots of room to play."

When Emily tried to put the box on the wagon it was too heavy. She could barely move it sideways.

"Box on wagon first," she said.

She laid the box on its side and the puppies crawled out. Then she put the box on the wagon, but quickly realized that holding a wriggling puppy in one arm and tilting the box with the other one didn't work as planned.

Frustrated, she plopped to the ground. The puppies swarmed over her, licking, nipping, climbing, and begging for attention. There had to be a better way to load them. She glanced around and saw an old plow near the fence. Maybe she could stand on it. Moving the puppies aside, she got up and hauled the box and wagon over to the plow. She balanced on top of it and peered inside the box. It was the perfect height for loading puppies.

A short time later, all the pups were back inside the box which was already on top of the wagon. Emily lay in the grass, her arms spread above her head. She was tired and thirsty, but happy this part of the rescue was over. Lilyanne curled up next to her.

Emily stroked the dog's neck. "I'll get your puppies to a safe place. I promise."

She rested a bit before heading home. The wagon rolled along nicely, but she had to stop a few times and shift the box to keep it steady.

During the walk back to her farm, the pups never stopped crying. Probably scared and hungry, she thought. Lilyanne paced nervously alongside, sniffing the box several times. She didn't seem very happy either.

The sun had touched the treetops when she unlatched the door to the old machinery barn. This would be the pups' new home. The barn was far enough away from the house, no one would find them. Emily peered inside. The old combine and tractor looked like big gray monsters watching her every move. Emily pulled the wagon up to the door, tilted the box over the threshold, and gave it a little shake. All at once the puppies tumbled out, squealing, onto the dirt floor. Lilyanne darted back and forth, barking.

"Go inside, girl," Emily coaxed. "You'll be safe here."

Cautiously, Lilyanne stepped inside the barn.

Emily followed and closed the door. Lilyanne dropped to the floor, panting heavily. The pups ran over to nurse. While they were busy, Emily tore apart the box and spread the pieces around. She found some dusty rags, shook them and laid them on the cardboard to make a bed. She tried to get Lilyanne to lie down on it, but she wouldn't move. Lilyanne looked exhausted, and even a bit sad. Emily didn't know what else to do for her.

"I have to go, but you'll be safe here." She stepped back, hands on hips, watching momma and her babies. She wanted to stay with them, but the rescue had taken longer than planned.

Emily stepped outside and latched the door. She rubbed her arms. The air had turned cooler. She hid the wagon in the weeds next to the barn and ran to the house. She sure hoped Mom and Dad had been delayed in town.

CHAPTER 4

Liar, Liar!

Slowly, Emily opened the screened door and crept inside. She took three steps and heard, "Where have you been, young lady?"

She nearly jumped out of her shoes. "Mom! You scared me."

Her mother grabbed her shoulders. "Where did you go? I specifically told you to stay near the house and you disobeyed me."

Emily fumbled for words. She couldn't tell the truth, not yet. "I took a walk."

Mom scowled. "This is the second time today you took off. I don't like it. Not one bit."

A car pulled up the driveway, and Mom went to the door.

"It's your father and grandfather. They've been looking for you. Now go to the kitchen and stay there."

Emily sat at the table, hugging herself. She didn't mean to be any trouble. Mom and Dad had Greg to worry about, and the broken-down truck. Her stomach was tied up in knots. Everything was all mixed up just because she wanted to help the puppies. But she had done it, and they were safe. That was the most important thing right now.

She eyed the plate of peanut butter cookies still sitting on the counter and wondered if Lilyanne would eat them. She swiped three cookies, wrapped them in a napkin and tucked them under her shirt. She'd have to find a lot more food for Lilyanne, but this was a start.

Outside, her parents talked with Grandpa. Dad was the loudest. He sure sounded mad. A few minutes later Grandpa's truck started up with a rumble. Emily hoped he wasn't mad at her.

Her parents entered the kitchen. Mom slid into a chair while Dad leaned against the wall. They stared at her. Emily felt hot and itchy all over.

"I thought you might have gone to find those puppies,"

Dad said. "I looked around Mr. Brock's barns. The hunting dogs were sure riled up. Were you there?"

Emily shook her head while her brain whispered *liar, liar.*

"We expect you to obey us," he added.

Emily couldn't look at him.

"You'll have extra chores tomorrow as punishment, and you will stay around the house all day. Do you understand?"

"Yes," Emily replied. "I'm sorry."

Dad turned and left the room.

Mom reached over and clasped Emily's hands. "You haven't been yourself lately. Is it because of Greg, or this puppy nonsense?"

"I don't know. Maybe both." Emily sighed. It felt good to say that out loud.

"It's hard not to worry about your brother," Mom said. "But we have to believe he's all right even when we don't hear from him. Remember how we were told that letters can take a long time to reach Greg, or for his to reach us? But we still need to write and pray our mail is getting to him." She sat back and rubbed her forehead.

"He's coming home soon, right?" Emily asked. She

wished she could go find Greg, just like she did the puppies. But her big brother was far away, across oceans and other countries. Emily felt the knot in the back of her throat as she wondered where Greg was at that moment. At least she knew where the puppies were, and that they were safe.

"We're hopeful Greg will be home soon. Now, it's been an exhausting day for all of us. And don't worry about those puppies. Mr. Brock will do what's right for them."

"Can I go to my room now?"

Mom nodded. "I think a bath is in order first."

Emily lay in the bathtub, thinking about all the things that had happened during the day from the mean Trenton sisters, to the news of the puppies, and then getting in trouble – twice. She mostly thought about the rescue, and her heart swelled. The pups were safe, and that was the best feeling.

After her bath, Emily put on her pajamas and brushed her teeth. But then she remembered she had to feed Lilyanne. How would she get food, without anyone noticing, and sneak out to the barn? It would have to happen after her parents went to sleep.

She needed something to do to pass the time. Emily sat at her desk and pulled paper and a pencil from the drawer. A letter was stuck to the paper, a letter from Greg. It was the last one he'd written her. She'd forgotten to put it with her other treasures in the hat box underneath her bed.

Emily unfolded the letter. It was dated July 6, but she hadn't received it until the first week of August. Slowly, she began to read.

Hi EM-Eeeeeeeee,

How's my favorite sister doing? Oh, yeah, you're my only sister. Well, you'd better be okay because I won't have it any other way. Not much has changed over here. We're on the move quite a bit. I hope my letters are reaching you. I'm thinking about you, and Mom, and Dad, always. I hope you had a fun 4ᵗʰ of July and that you went to Freeland's community picnic. The food we get is boring (tell Mom to send more care packages. Hint! Hint). I'm having trouble remembering what a good hot dog should taste like. When I get home, the first thing I'm going to do is take Queenie for a nice, long, QUIET walk. Here's a pinch for your arm because I know you miss my pinches.

Love from your one and only brother,

Greg

Emily's heartbeat double-flipped when she read the sentence about Queenie. Her lip quivered. Someone should tell him that Queenie died. He deserved to know. She picked up her pencil.

Hi Greg-eeeeeeeeee,

I hope you are okay because we are worried. We haven't got a letter in a long, long time. When are you coming home? Mom said you need to tell us the date. Please tell us. We can't wait to see you. The Trenton sisters are still mean to me. I try to ignore them like you told me to, but it's hard. Have you seen Paul? Did he tell you Lilyanne had puppies? Mr. Brock says they're mutts and not worth anything, but I don't believe it. I have something to tell you. It's important.

Emily paused, ready to spill the beans, but found she couldn't write the words. To tell him would be defying her parents. And he would know that she hadn't kept Queenie safe, like she'd promised. Mom had been right all along. The sad news should wait for Greg to get home. She erased her last two sentences and wrote:

I saved Lilyanne's puppies today. I brought them to our farm with a box and a wagon. I took the trail by the river and hid the pups in the machinery barn. When you get back, I'll tell you all about the rescue. It was hard work, but I'm glad I did it. The puppies are safe now. I hope I get to keep them. Even one would be nice. I like Pumpkin the best. She's small like me. Please come home soon.

Love, Emily

She folded the letter and taped every side so that only her brother could read it. Her door opened, and Mom stepped in.

"It's past your bedtime. What are you doing?"

"I wrote to Greg."

Mom's smiled, but the smile didn't fill her face like when she was happy.

"Well, off to bed," she said. "You have a lot of chores to do tomorrow, plus homework."

"Ok," Emily said. She put away her letter and climbed into bed.

***

It was a long time before deep snoring drifted from her parent's room. Emily padded across the floor, grabbed the cookies and crept downstairs. The stairs creaked, and she sucked in her breath and waited. There was no noise from Mom and Dad's room. That was good. Three more steps, two steps, one.

She moved quickly into the kitchen. The cookies went into a paper sack along with a few slices of bread and a partial box of cereal. She pulled on her shoes, grabbed a flashlight and slid out the door. A full moon lit up the yard as she ran through the grass toward the barn. Bats flew overhead. Emily covered her head and ducked. She didn't want them tangling up in her hair. An owl hooted from the river, and the sound echoed. Goosebumps marched up and down her arms, but she gulped down her fear and kept her mind on Lilyanne.

She stepped inside the dark barn. It was cold and quiet. Emily shined the flashlight around but didn't see Lilyanne or the pups.

"Lilyanne? Where are you?" She bent over and shined the light under one of the tractors.

Lilyanne's eyes glowed back as she crawled out from under it and sniffed the sack of food. The pups staggered to their feet, whining something awful.

Emily shushed them. "If you keep making noise, everyone will know you're here." Softly, she sang three rounds of *Twinkle, Twinkle Little Star* which, surprisingly, settled them down.

She ripped open the sack and dumped all the food on top of it. It only took Lilyanne a few minutes to eat it all. Emily wished she had more.

"I hope you don't get a stomachache," she said. "I'll be back in the morning."

She stepped outside and latched the door. From the pond, a chorus of frogs filled the night air. Looking up, she saw a night sky full of stars. By the time she reached the house her shoes were soaked from the dew on the grass. Emily took them off, carried them up the stairs and tossed them under her desk.

Shivering, she climbed into bed. As she snuggled under her covers, she grinned. Lilyanne had a full belly, and her puppies were nursing. Emily yawned something fierce and promptly fell asleep.

CHAPTER 5

Taking Care of Puppies

The next morning Emily rolled over and stretched.

"Ow!" Her whole body ached. Probably from the puppy rescue, she thought. Loading the rocks and the puppies had been hard work.

Slowly, she moved her legs and arms as if making a snow angel. Each time she did so she felt better. Kitchen sounds floated up the stairs. She smelled bacon. Yum. Saturday breakfasts were the best.

And then she remembered her promise to Lilyanne. Emily jumped out of bed, pulled on some clothes and flew downstairs. She skidded to a stop in the kitchen when she saw her mom at the sink. She wouldn't be able to swipe food from the pantry now.

Mom turned. "Hi, honey. How are you today?"

"Good," Emily said, stretching. "But I'm a little sore. I think I worked too hard yesterday."

Mom put a hand on Emily's forehead. "No fever. Dad said you were collecting rocks. What are you going to do with them?"

"Umm, I don't know." She wished Mom hadn't asked. She didn't want to lie, but what could she say? Suddenly, she had a great idea. "I could put them around Queenie's grave." Queenie had been buried next to the orchard. Emily had planted flowers there, but the grave didn't have a marker.

Mom's expression softened before she turned to the sink. "That would be a nice way to honor her."

The room was awfully quiet. The grandfather clock in the dining room seemed to tick-tock louder than normal.

"Mom?"

"Hmm?"

"Are you thinking about Greg?"

"All the time. It's hard waiting for his letters. Keeping

busy helps a lot, though." She turned and grabbed Emily's hands. "So why don't you bring me your letter and I'll send it today. It will cheer us both up."

"Okay." Emily raced to her room and returned with the letter.

"What's with the tape?" Mom asked when Emily handed it over.

Emily blushed. "It's private."

"Oh, I see. Well, let's get on with our day." Mom moved Emily's schoolbooks and a pencil from the counter to the table. "Homework first, followed by chores."

Emily stared at her social studies and arithmetic books. She couldn't do homework now. Lilyanne needed her. "Can I do something else first?"

Mom stared at her, hands on hips. "I can't believe you are asking me that, after what happened last night. The answer is no."

Emily slumped in the chair. There was no arguing with Mom. Lilyanne would have to wait. She opened her arithmetic book, picked up the pencil and turned to page twenty-one.

A little while later, a plate of scrambled eggs, toast and bacon appeared in front of her. Emily's mouth watered.

"Thanks, Mom!"

"You're welcome, but don't think you're off the hook from last night. After Mr. Jones fixes the truck, your father has a delivery to finish. He wants to talk to you when he gets back."

"Is he mad?"

"He's concerned," Mom corrected. "I've got my own chores to do now. Let me know when you've finished your homework."

Emily took a bite of toast, but couldn't enjoy her food knowing Lilyanne was starving. She put her breakfast in a dish towel and hid everything behind a chair in the mudroom. Hurrying through her homework, Emily finished in less than an hour. After she put her plate in the sink, she read her list of chores.

1. Pull weeds in flower gardens and water flowers

2. Beat rugs

3. Sweep, dust and organize bedroom

At least now she was able to leave the house. She could feed Lilyanne before doing her chores. Upstairs, Mom hummed while cleaning.

Emily stood on the bottom step and called out, "Mom!

I'm going outside to weed the flower gardens."

"Okay," came the reply.

Emily grabbed a plate from the cupboard. She found a can of baked beans in the pantry, and the can opener in the drawer. Everything went into a grocery sack along with the wrapped breakfast food. She looked for her shoes, but remembered they were wet and still under her desk. She dug out an old pair from the shoe bin. As soon as she left the house, she heard the puppies. Their barking was faint, but she could hear them. She sprinted toward the machinery barn, lifted the latch and stepped inside.

PHEW! Emily pinched her nose and her eyes watered. Ick. Dog poop. She hadn't thought about that. Slowly, her eyes adjusted to the cracks of sunlight streaming through the walls.

Lilyanne paced, her sides heaving. The door had scratch marks all over it, and there was a large hole nearby. It looked as if she'd had spent the whole night trying to escape.

"Come here girl," Emily said, still pinching her nose.

Lilyanne limped over followed closely by whining pups.

"I'll take care of you," she said, scratching Lilyanne's ears. "I promise."

She fed Lilyanne the breakfast items, and then opened the

beans and dumped them onto the plate. Emily tried to keep the pups away so their momma could eat, but it wasn't easy. In seconds, Lilyanne had finished and nudged Emily's leg with her nose.

"What do you want, girl?"

Lilyanne turned away and paced some more.

Water! How could she have forgotten that? She eased outside, pushing the pups back inside with her foot as they tried to escape.

In a roundabout fashion, Emily made her way to the pump near the house. She stayed hidden as much as possible. She pumped until the pail was a third full, and then ran back to the barn taking the same route. When she set the pail down, Lilyanne drank until full and then limped over to the rags. She turned in a circle three times and curled up in a ball.

The pups scrambled over each other to reach their mother. Two of them tipped over the water bucket, spooked themselves, and scooted beneath the threshing machine. But soon they all settled down beside Lilyanne and a few pups began to nurse.

A soft humming from bees in the rafters filled the barn. Emily imagined the newspaper headlines reading BRAVE

GIRL PULLS OFF AMAZING PUPPY RESCUE, or something like that. Too bad the Trenton sisters hadn't seen her in action, she thought. They wouldn't call her teeny, short stuff or freckled shrimp if they knew what she'd done.

Emily pulled her shirt up to her nose and breathed through it. There was a lot of poop. The barn smelled worse by the second. She'd have to clean it up now.

While the pups snoozed, Emily opened the barn door to let in fresh air. She wished she had a shovel to use as a scoop. Instead, she used a small piece of wood to push the poop into the pail. She gasped from the smell, turned away and took a shallow breath and then continued. On her next trip to the barn she'd bring a shovel and wooden clothes pins for her nose.

It was time to leave as her chores were waiting. Emily crept outside and latched the door. She dumped the poop in the weeds far from the barn and rinsed the pail at the pump before dashing to the flower gardens.

Emily sang as she pulled weeds. Rescuing the puppies felt good. So good she thought she'd burst. Taking care of them would be a big job, but she could do it. The toughest part would be keeping them a secret.

She finished weeding and watering and moved on to her next chore. Four rugs hung on the clothesline waiting for her.

Emily grabbed the corn broom and beat each rug several times, which caused her to sneeze several times.

Her bedroom was the last item on her chore list. It took about an hour to arrange her stuffed animals, organize her drawing supplies, dust and sweep the floor. Mom came in and gave the room the "white glove" test.

"Well done, Emily. You can go play, but please don't leave the farm."

"I won't," Emily said. She ran downstairs to call Sarah. She picked up the phone and heard a voice on the line.

"The phone is in use," said their neighbor, Mrs. Leaman.

"Sorry," Emily mumbled and hung up. Party lines were frustrating when she wanted to talk to Sarah right then. She wished they had their own phone line.

She went to the kitchen and opened the refrigerator. She saw a leftover ham and a chunk of cheese on the shelf, something wrapped in paper, and potato salad. Probably food Mom was saving for lunch. She'd notice if it was gone.

Emily returned to the pantry. What could she take this time? A can of green beans, a can of corn, and a sleeve of saltine crackers went into a brown paper sack. She found an old comb under the bathroom sink and added it to the sack.

Lilyanne's matted coat really needed to be brushed.

Emily tried the phone again. This time the line was available, and she dialed Sarah's number.

"Hello?"

"Hi, Aunt Chris," Emily said.

"Emily! It's good to hear from you. What are you doing today?"

"Cleaning and weeding. Can I talk to Sarah?"

"She's not here, dear. She's with her dad this weekend. I'm sorry."

"When will she be home?"

"Not until Sunday afternoon. Can I help you with anything?"

"No, that's okay. Please tell her I called."

"I will, dear. Put your mother on the phone. We haven't chatted in two days."

"Okay. Bye." She set the phone on the counter and ran to the stairs. "Mom! Aunt Chris wants to talk to you."

Emily grabbed the bag of food and slipped out the door. She zigzagged her way across the yard in case Mom was watching. As she passed by the clothesline, she pulled off two wooden clothes pins.

The pups were piled up by the door when she entered the barn. Phew! It smelled worse than before. Emily pinched a clothes pin on her nose to block the stink. Lilyanne sniffed the bag of food, acting like she would tear into it any second. Emily opened the cans and dumped the food. Lilyanne gobbled everything and nudged her for more.

Emily's eyes watered so much she could barely see. She stepped outside, latched the door, and pulled off the clothes pin. She plopped at the trunk of a Maple tree and leaned back. Taking care of Lilyanne, and the pups, was a lot harder than she'd thought it would be. She couldn't keep raiding the kitchen. And the never-ending poop was a big problem.

Emily needed more than a shovel. She needed big time help, and it had to be someone who would keep the pups a secret. But who?

CHAPTER 6

Guilty

Emily sat against the Maple tree for a long time, worrying about how to care for the puppies. They were a handful and she realized she needed a lot of help. Greg was her first choice, but he was a long way from home. Her history teacher had showed her the world map and pointed to Vietnam. Emily remembered thinking Greg might as well be on the moon.

She'd ask Sarah, but her cousin had enough trouble trying to keep track of whose house she would be at each weekend. Uncle Tim lived three hours away now. Ever since her aunt and uncle had separated, Emily hardly saw Sarah. And the last time they'd talked, her cousin told her she hated packing her suitcase and going from one home to another. Emily couldn't imagine doing that. She could only see her room, her house, her family.

She decided to ask Grandpa for help. There was nobody else she could trust. He was the one who wanted her to have a dog. He would be happy she rescued the puppies.

Emily got back to work. She carried more water from the pump and gave Lilyanne a drink. After that, she took the comb and worked on Lilyanne's coat, clearing tangles and removing clumps of dirt. Lilyanne looked prettier now that she was all fluffed up.

Grandpa's truck was parked in the driveway when she got back to the house. Emily's heart did a little skip. If he agreed to help, they could go to town right away and buy dog food for Lilyanne.

Emily entered the kitchen. Mom was making sandwiches at the table as Grandpa sliced pickles.

"There you are," Mom said. "I was about to call you for lunch."

"Those sandwiches look good," Emily said. "I'm starving. Are you starving, Grandpa?" She rubbed her clammy hands against her shirt. Why was she so nervous?

"I'm a little hungry," he replied. His answer was short,

and he didn't give her the usual wink.

Emily poured a glass of milk and sat at the table. No one said a word as they ate.

"Are you feeling okay, Henry?" Mom asked.

"Feeling fine," Grandpa answered. He continued to eat his sandwich.

Emily dunked a graham cracker. She chewed slowly. Grandpa seemed different, and that made her feel all jumbled inside.

A few minutes later, he pushed back from the table. "Thanks for the lunch, Clara. I'm going to work on the garden tractor now." He tapped Emily on the shoulder. "I'll see you in the garage when you're done."

Emily watched him leave. He hadn't asked her to come to the garage; he'd told her to. *Something's wrong!* She would have gone after him right then, but Mom made her eat the whole sandwich.

She gobbled it down. "Can I go now?"

Mom nodded. Emily put her lunch plate in the sink and rushed to the garage.

Grandpa held the valve end of a grease pump against a tractor wheel. Emily waited for him to finish. For the first time in her life, she felt tongue-tied around him.

"Lilyanne disappeared yesterday," He said as he worked. "Mr. Brock thinks someone took her and the pups."

A lump grew in Emily's throat. She swallowed hard, but the lump remained.

"He's been putting out food and water," Grandpa added. "Lilyanne didn't eat any of it last night."

"But Mr. Brock doesn't care about those puppies," Emily said.

"It may seem like he doesn't care, but I know he wants them. A person ought to think twice before stealing another man's dogs."

Stealing? The word stabbed Emily square in the middle of her heart. She hadn't stolen the pups, or Lilyanne. She'd protected them. And she couldn't have stopped Lilyanne from following. Her eyes darted to Grandpa.

"I-I wonder who took them," she stammered. Her face and neck grew hot and clammy. Every lie that left her mouth made her feel worse. She looked into Grandpa's eyes and knew that he knew she'd lied. She had to leave. She had to get away from Grandpa and away from her lies. She fled toward the barn and the puppies.

By the time she reached the machinery barn, she was filled with guilt. Grandpa was right. She'd stolen the puppies and Lilyanne.

She unlatched the door and stepped inside. The puppies were sleeping, piled on top of each other. Lilyanne cocked her head but didn't get up. And in a quick second Emily's puppy world was okay again. She loved the puppies, and Lilyanne. They were part of her life now.

"I'm going to give you names," Emily whispered. The multi-colored pup she called Splotches. There was Goldie, Sandy, Brownie, Rusty and Caramel – all named for their colors. A female pup she called Sarah. The one with white whiskers became Henry, in honor of Grandpa. The largest puppy, who pushed his brothers and sisters around, she named Bruiser. And the last, the smallest and her favorite, was Pumpkin.

Two of the pups shifted beside their mother, trying to nurse. Lilyanne jumped to her feet and side-stepped them. Now all the pups were awake, following their mother wherever she went. But Lilyanne kept moving away from them, and Emily didn't understand why.

The pups cried louder and louder. Suddenly, Lilyanne turned toward the door, stiffened and growled. At the same time, Emily heard a noise outside. Her heart pounded as she shushed the puppies, but they wouldn't stop crying.

She held her breath and stared at the latch. Slowly, it moved upward. Go away, she prayed. The door creaked open. Her heart thumped, thumped, thumped.

Grandpa stepped inside, leaned back against the door frame and crossed his arms. He chewed slowly on a toothpick, working it up and down. "I knew the pups were here, Emmy. I never thought you'd lie to me."

Emily took a deep breath. "I wanted to tell you, but you said someone stole the pups and I didn't steal them. I rescued them." She tried to hold back the tears, but they came anyway.

"You didn't have to lie to me."

"I-I know," Emily choked.

Grandpa opened his arms. "Come here, girl."

Emily melted into his embrace. She hiccupped as she tried to catch her breath. "Lilyanne's hungry all the time. She needs a lot more food."

"A momma dog needs extra food when she's nursing," Grandpa said. He rubbed Emily's back. "I'll help you, but we need to do what's right. And that means we have to take them all back to Mr. Brock."

Emily stiffened. "I won't take them back. I promised Lilyanne."

"Emmy," Grandpa said quietly. "It's the right thing to do."

She didn't answer right away, thinking it through.

"He'll hate me for taking Lilyanne."

"He won't. He'll be happy to have her back," Grandpa said. "I want to tell you something. Mr. Brock isn't a mean person. He has a lot on his mind right now, and the pups are not at the top of the list. Remember, he's worried about Paul the same as we are about Greg."

Emily stared at the dirt floor. She hadn't thought about that. Of course, Mr. Brock would be worried about Paul.

"And," Grandpa continued, "I'm convinced he won't hurt the pups. We'll take one step at a time. First, we must tell your parents. Your dad came home a few minutes ago. It's as good a time as any for a confession. And then we'll load up Lilyanne and the pups and clean up this floor. It sure stinks in here."

"Not as much as it did earlier," Emily said.

Grandpa opened the door. "Are you coming?"

"In a minute." Emily dreaded telling her parents. But maybe they'd listen to her, see the puppies and fall in love with them, too. Maybe. She spent another minute or two with the pups, put on a brave face and stepped out of the barn.

Ten minutes later, Emily had finished her puppy rescue story. Mom sat there, rigid, with the biggest frown on her face. "Did you take food from the kitchen to feed those dogs?"

Emily nodded. "It was for Lilyanne."

"You may have meant well," Mom said, "but all this time you lied about where you were and what you were doing."

Emily stared at the flowers in the wallpaper. She didn't know what to say.

Dad leaned against the kitchen wall, rubbing his chin. "I can't believe you brought the puppies here. And Lilyanne."

"You might as well be mad at me, too," Grandpa said.

Dad took a deep breath. "I'm not mad. I'm upset. We have to make it right with Mr. Brock." He grabbed a chair and sat. "I can't believe this happened."

Emily couldn't keep quiet any longer. "I wanted to help them."

"But you didn't think it through," Dad said. "You didn't talk to us, and you didn't think about the consequences. Those pups are going back immediately."

She received "the look," which meant don't argue with me.

"Okay," Emily whispered.

"She won't have to go alone." Grandpa arose from his chair. "I started this whole mess and I'll help finish it."

Dad nodded and crossed his arms. "When you come back, I want you both to forget about this puppy nonsense. There will be no more discussions over them or any other dog. Ever."

CHAPTER 7

Puppy Predicament

Emily ran straight to the puppies. Her heart ached. She didn't want to take them back to Mr. Brock. Inside the barn, the little rascals chased each other around, skidding on the floor. She picked up Splotches and Goldie, snuggled them and kissed their noses.

The door opened and Grandpa stepped inside.

"You okay?" he asked.

"Not really."

"Emmy, we need to fix our wrongs. And good can come from bad. First things first, let's get momma outside and away from her pups for a few minutes. She needs a break."

Emily called Lilyanne over to the door. She side-stepped her pups and dashed from the barn while Emily shooed the pups back. Quickly, she stepped outside and closed the door. Their yelps made it clear they weren't happy to be left behind.

Grandpa lifted a bag of dog food from the truck bed and swung it to the ground.

"You bought food!" Emily clapped her hands. "Thank you!"

"Can't take back hungry dogs." Grandpa opened the bag, scooped out a small bowl of food and set it down. Within seconds, Lilyanne gobbled up every piece of food.

"My, she's a hungry dog," he said.

"So are the puppies," Emily answered.

Grandpa poured another half bowl of food. Lilyanne devoured it and looked as if she could eat more. And when Grandpa gave her water, she lapped up every drop.

He rubbed Lilyanne's neck. "Now that you're fed, we're going to teach your pups you aren't the only source of food."

"I thought they couldn't eat dog food," Emily said.

"They won't do well with hard food. We'll soften it up a little."

They took the food and water inside the barn, but left Lilyanne outside. Grandpa put a small amount of food into the dish and added a little bit of water. "Let it sit a bit."

While they waited, Emily held Bruiser to keep him from bullying his brothers and sisters. "Give it a stir now, Emmy. Let's see what they think of their new food."

She stirred the food with her finger until it turned into a thick mush. It felt like cold oatmeal. She tasted it and quickly spit it out. *Yuck!* It stuck to her tongue and smelled like garbage. When she set the bowl down, the pups sniffed the food and walked around it. Bruiser and Caramel stepped into it, but none of the pups would eat the mush.

Emily picked up Henry and scooped mush onto her finger. He looked at it, but that was all. Grandpa held Sandy and gently pushed some into her mouth. She seemed to like it. They put the pups on the ground and, surprisingly, they began to eat from the bowl. Pretty soon all the pups were eating, and the mush turned into a mess. Everywhere! It was on their paws and tails and all over their faces.

Emily couldn't stop giggling as the pups licked each other.

"Well?" Grandpa asked.

Emily looked at him. "What?"

"You know what. It's time to take them back."

"I know," she replied, feeling sick about it.

Grandpa handed her a rag. "Come on. Let's make them presentable."

They cleaned the pups and put them in the back of the truck. Grandpa opened the barn door and windows to let in fresh air.

"We don't have time right now to clean the floor, but later you and I will have to do it. Do I have your promise you'll help me?"

Emily nodded, then asked, "Lilyanne doesn't want to nurse anymore," Emily said. "She's really skinny. Do you think she might be sick?"

"The pups are getting pretty big," he answered. "I think she's trying to wean them. If so, they'll need a lot more food from now on."

"Do you think Mr. Brock will feed them?"

"I'm sure he will," Grandpa said. "You need to stop worrying. The pups will be fine." He ruffled her hair. "Let's get going."

She couldn't, wouldn't, stop worrying. But when Grandpa walked to the truck, she knew she had to follow.

"Do you want to ride with them?" he asked.

Emily nodded, and Grandpa lowered the tailgate and boosted her inside. Lilyanne jumped in and poked her nose into each puppy, one by one, as if counting them. When Grandpa slammed the tailgate, Emily's skin prickled. She closed her eyes. No turning back now.

A few minutes later they pulled into Mr. Brock's driveway. Grandpa parked and got out. "Go tell him why we're here."

Emily climbed down, but once her feet touched the ground she froze. Her heart raced; she could barely breathe.

"Go on," Grandpa urged.

I can't, Emily thought. I won't. I can't. This isn't fair. She willed her feet to move, but they wouldn't.

"You can do this," Grandpa said.

She took a deep breath, shuffled over to the house and climbed the steps. Her stomach twisted and flipped. She turned toward the truck, pleading for Grandpa to help, but he wasn't looking her way.

Emily rapped lightly on the door. A few seconds later, she

heard heavy footsteps and Mr. Brock came to the screen door. He used a cane for support, which, for a second, surprised Emily. But then she remembered Grandpa saying Mr. Brock's leg hadn't healed right.

"Hello, Emily. What brings you by? I see your Grandpa's with you." He opened the door and called, "Afternoon, Henry."

"Howdy, Winston," Grandpa said.

Mr. Brock joined her on the porch. "Is that my Lilyanne in the truck bed?"

Emily scuffed her shoe and stared at the porch floor. Finally, in a quiet voice, she said, "Yes. Lilyanne and her puppies."

Mr. Brock leaned against the house. "I thought she was a goner. She's a mighty fine hunting dog and I wouldn't want to lose her. Where'd you find her?"

"In the old shed down the lane," Emily answered. "I was only going to take the puppies, but Lilyanne followed."

"I see," he said. "Do you think it's okay to take something that isn't yours?"

Emily felt her face grow hot. She hung her head and shoved her hands in her back pockets, wishing she could hide somewhere. "Um, no. It's not okay," she said softly.

"Then we agree. Now, let's get my girl from the truck."

She waited until Mr. Brock slowly made his way down the steps before she followed.

"Sorry about this, Winston," Grandpa said as the two men shook hands. "Emily's a good girl, but she got a little carried away over those pups."

Mr. Brock looked in the truck bed. "Don't know why anyone would care about them."

Emily pressed her lips together and glared at the ground. *I care!*

Grandpa lowered the tailgate and Lilyanne jumped down. He quickly shut it so the pups couldn't get out. Lilyanne circled the truck before sitting beside Grandpa. Emily noticed Mr. Brock didn't pet Lilyanne. Maybe he couldn't bend over with his cane, she thought. But still, he didn't even look at his dog.

"Don't know what to do with these pups," Mr. Brock said. "It's too bad they're mutts. They aren't worth their keep."

"Yes, they are!" The words burst from Emily's mouth like angry bees protecting their hive. "You can't hurt them."

"Emmy," Grandpa said sternly.

"Wait a minute," Mr. Brock said. "I wouldn't hurt a dog. Not even a mutt."

Emily wasn't listening. "Someone will want the puppies," she said. "I'll find homes for them."

Grandpa put a hand on her shoulder. "Calm down."

Mr. Brock frowned and rubbed his chin. "I don't have time for these puppies. If Paul were here, things would be different."

"Please, Mr. Brock. Please let me try."

No one spoke for a few seconds, and then Mr. Brock looked at Grandpa. "You know, Henry, with Lilyanne's good bloodline the pups might be worth, say, two dollars each."

Grandpa frowned. "A minute ago, you said they weren't worth anything."

"Well, they aren't to me," Mr. Brock said, "but they could make a good family dog. They should be weaned in a week or so, and ready to leave their mama."

"She's weaning them now," Emily said, praying he'd let her take them.

Mr. Brock stared at her, which made her squirm.

Please, please, please, Emily silently begged.

"All right," he said. "I'll let you try and find homes for them."

Grandpa's face turned red. "Go to the porch, Emmy."

"But Grandpa, I want to do this."

He pointed. "To the porch!"

Emily mumbled angrily all the way there and sat hard on the step. Luckily, she could still hear them talking.

"Be reasonable, Winston. It could be difficult to sell the puppies," Grandpa said.

"I know that, but your granddaughter could learn something from this," Mr. Brock said. "I'll give her one week beginning next Saturday. Pups that don't sell come back to me. When Paul returns, he can help me train them into hunters."

Emily heard the pups in the truck bed crying for their mother. Or maybe they were crying for help.

Grandpa motioned for her to come back. "Get in the truck, Emmy."

She climbed into the front seat and waited for him. A few minutes later, he got in and sat there, hands gripping the steering wheel.

"Please don't be mad, Grandpa. I just want to help the

puppies."

"We can figure this out." He started the truck and shifted into gear. "The pups and Lilyanne will stay in the old chicken coop for now. We'll get them settled and fed. After that, it looks like we will be having another discussion with your parents. We might as well get it over with."

Emily swallowed hard. Talking to her parents, again, wasn't something she wanted to do.

Not at all.

CHAPTER 8

A Plan for Puppies

"No!" Dad said. "Absolutely not."

"Let me explain," Grandpa argued. "I think this will be good for Emily, and the puppies. It could all work out for the best."

Emily sat on the floor of her bedroom, next to the slightly opened door, eavesdropping on their conversation. She'd been sent to her room as soon as Mom and Dad had heard about Mr. Brock's decision.

"I don't know what's gotten into her lately," Mom said.

They talked some more, but Emily couldn't hear them clearly. They must have moved into the kitchen. She heard the screened door slam. Dashing to the window, she saw Grandpa climb into his truck and drive away.

Emily fell back on her bed and stared at the ceiling. She wanted to tell Mom and Dad there was nothing wrong with her. She simply wanted to help the puppies.

The door opened. Mom stepped inside. "We need to talk."

Emily sat up. "Okay."

Mom wasn't smiling as she perched on the bed.

Emily fidgeted with her bedspread. "Are you mad at me?"

"You are such a determined young lady," Mom answered. She reached out and pushed Emily's bangs to one side.

"I am?"

"When it comes to some things, like these puppies, you are."

"I only want them to be safe, Mom. When you see them, you'll love them."

"The puppies are lucky to have you on their side," she said, taking hold of Emily's hands.

"What does that mean?"

"It means your father and I have agreed to let you sell them."

Emily got on her knees and bounced on the bed. "Really?"

"This is the only way to make things right with Mr. Brock. And we know you won't be happy until the puppies have new homes."

Emily hugged Mom. "Thank you."

"I want you to learn something from this, honey. We are the parents, and we make the decisions for our family. One day, when you are a parent, you'll understand why."

Emily nodded, not exactly sure what Mom meant but felt it best to agree.

"Now, let's have our dinner. We'll be eating in shifts tonight and it's already after seven o'clock."

Emily followed her to the stairs. "I saw Grandpa leave. He looked upset."

"He is, but not with you. Your dad went after him. I think they need a little time to talk things over."

After dinner, Emily went back to her room. She sat at the desk and pulled paper and a pencil from her drawer. She drew a picture of what should be ten little puppies playing in the yard. Instead, they looked like ten little blobs doing nothing. She wadded up the paper, tossed it to her wastebasket and drew them again. The girl puppies had ribbons in their hair.

She drew the boy puppies barking at each other.

A knock on the door startled her.

"Can I come in?" Dad asked.

"Yes."

He came beside her. "What are you drawing?"

Emily covered the paper with her hand. "Oh, nothing."

"Looks like puppies," he said. "That doesn't surprise me."

"It's not very good."

"I can tell the girls from the boys," Dad said. "Your mom and I are watching television. Do you want to join us?"

Emily shook her head. "I'm tired."

"Okay," he said. "But come on down if you change your mind."

Before he turned away Emily grabbed his arm. "Are you still mad at me?"

He patted her shoulder. "No, I'm not. But I want you to do the best you can for the puppies. You do that, okay? And we'll help you if you need us."

"Thanks, Dad. I will. I promise."

After he left Emily changed into her pajamas and climbed

into bed. She wondered if the puppies were playing, or sleeping, or getting into trouble. Soon they'd have new owners; people who would love them and care for them.

"Night, night, puppies," she whispered.

* * *

After church on Sunday, Emily spent an hour making posters. They had to be done right so people would want to buy Lilyanne's pups. She closed her eyes and thought about what Greg would write. He would say, "Get to the point, Emily."

In large letters she wrote:

TEN PUPPIES FOR SALE

Cute and cuddly

Mother: Golden Retriever and good hunter

Call 555-0110

Emily drew puppy pictures on the top and bottom. When she'd finished three posters, she went to find Dad. He'd promised to take her to town to put the posters in store windows. He was in the garage with the truck hood propped open and grease up to his elbows.

"I finished the posters," Emily said. "Can we leave soon?"

"I need a few minutes to clean up. Go tell your mother.

We're going to have lunch at Frannie's."

"Oh, boy," Emily whooped. Frannie had the best food in town. Her pies were known as "first prize" pies.

Fifteen minutes later they were on their way. Dad drove slowly with the windows down. The warm autumn air filled the car with smells of ripe gardens. As they drove past Mr. Brock's farm, Emily stuck her head out the window hoping to see the puppies. She wondered if they missed her as much as she missed them. The pups weren't in the yard, though. Neither was Mr. Brock. Emily slid back in her seat. She hoped he was taking good care of them. She decided right then to check on the pups as soon as possible to make sure they were okay.

As they passed by the Freeland Feed and Grain, Emily noticed the parking lot was filled with trucks and tractors.

"I wonder what's going on," Dad said.

"That's strange," Mom replied. "Jim isn't open on Sundays."

Dad parked along the sidewalk. "I'll check it out. Do you want to wait for me?"

Emily's tummy rumbled. "I'm hungry."

"We'll meet you at Frannie's," Mom said. "Come on,

Emily. Let's stretch our legs."

"I might as well take a poster with me," Dad said. "Maybe Jim will put it up somewhere."

Emily took another poster with her to Frannie's. As soon as they walked through the door, Frannie put down the coffee pot she carried and gave them big hugs.

"What do you have there," she asked Emily.

She showed Frannie the poster. "I'm selling puppies. Can I put this in your window?"

"Well, where did you get puppies," she asked, looking confused.

"The pups belong to Winston Brock," Mom answered.

"Oh, I see," Frannie said. "Now grab the last table over in the corner. I'll take care of this poster." Frannie showed it to her customers. She'd point to Emily, to the poster, and back to Emily. Emily blushed as people looked her way.

When Dad arrived, Frannie followed him to their table. She pulled out her order form.

"What 'cha having today, Emily?" she asked.

"Macaroni and cheese, please, and milk."

"Is that all?" Frannie asked.

"Oh, and bacon on the side," Emily answered.

"Bacon on the side. Got it!"

Dad ordered chicken pot pie, his favorite meal. Mom chose the same and Frannie scurried off toward the kitchen. Mom opened her napkin and slid it onto her lap. "What on earth was going on at the Feed and Grain?"

"It was the annual meeting about small game hunting," Dad said, chuckling. "I should have guessed that by the trucks parked there. Lots of hunters."

"Will Mr. Hicks put up my poster?" Emily asked.

He nodded. "But don't get your hopes up. We'll see what happens."

A short time later, Frannie brought their food. Emily dove into the homemade macaroni and cheese. It was delicious. She shoveled it in, her mind already on dessert. They always had pie after their meal, and she wondered what kind she'd get today. Frannie baked many varieties, and she usually brought them the pie of the day.

Emily waited patiently for Mom and Dad to finish their meals. When they weren't looking, she slipped the bacon into the napkin on her lap. It would be her treat for Lilyanne for the next time she saw her.

After what seemed like forever Frannie showed up with three plates of peach pie. She passed them out and pulled up a chair between Emily and Mom. Emily forked a big piece into her mouth while the two women leaned close to each other.

"Did you get a letter?" Frannie asked.

Emil's fork hung over her pie as she listened.

"No. It's been three weeks now, the longest time with no mail. I need to know Greg's okay."

"Of course, dear." Frannie said. "You'll get a letter any day now. You'll see."

"I'm trying to stay positive," Mom said. "It's not easy."

Abruptly, Dad cleared his throat and pushed back from the table. "We have to get going. I'll take the bill now, Frannie, and wrap the pies to go, please."

"Yes," Mom said. "We should be heading on home."

While Frannie headed toward the kitchen, Emily laid down her fork. She wasn't hungry anymore.

They walked to the car. Mom and Dad were unusually quiet. Emily thought it must have something to do with Frannie's question about letters from Greg. He was on everyone's mind right now. *Please send us a letter this week,* she prayed. *You need to cheer up Mom and Dad. And me, too.*

She decided to send him the puppy picture she'd drawn.

The last stop of the day was the grocery store. The store's big front window overflowed with notices like bake sales, farm equipment and animals for sale. Emily was certain Mr. Fripp would put her poster in the window.

Dad waited in the car while Mom shopped for a few groceries. Emily helped Mr. Fripp tape up the poster.

"I hear these pups belong to Winston Brock," Mr. Fripp said.

She nodded. "Lilyanne is the mother. She's a prize hunting dog."

"But the puppies aren't purebred?" Mr. Fripp asked.

"They're a mixed breed," Emily said. She refused to call them mutts. "I sure hope people come and see them."

Mom joined them. "Time to go, Emily."

"Well, good luck selling the puppies," Mr. Fripp said.

"Thanks," Emily answered. She left the store filled with hope.

On the way home, they passed by the Trenton house. Emily saw Sissy and Carol out in the yard. But there was no sign of their dogs, Captain and Molly. Come to think of it, she couldn't remember the last time she'd seen their dogs. It's not fair, she thought. They have two dogs and never play with them. She wanted one dog, just one.

They were almost to Mr. Brock's farm when a car pulled out of his driveway and passed them. With a gasp, Mom grabbed Dad's arm.

"What is it, Clara?" Dad asked, turning her way.

Emily leaned over the front seat. "What's the matter?"

"The driver." Mom's voice was almost a whisper. "He stared at me, and he looked like he was in shock. Something's going on at Winston's."

Dad stiffened. "Like what?"

"What is it? What's wrong?" Emily asked again.

"Emily, calm down and sit back in your seat please," Dad said firmly.

Frustrated, Emily slid back. Her parents were hiding something from her, and it had to do with the person in that car.

CHAPTER 9

Something to Talk About

Dad had barely parked when Emily jumped from the car and ran off toward the tire swing. She wanted to be alone to think. Mom and Dad were hiding something, she knew it. She felt all jumpy inside.

Halfway to the swing she slowed and then stopped. Running away wouldn't do any good. She needed to stay near her parents to learn what was going on. Emily spun around and what she saw made her stomach flip flop. Mom and Dad were holding hands as they went into the house. They never held hands. Well, not never, but only for important things, or bad things. Like when Queenie died, and when Greg went to war.

Emily raced back to the house and crouched beneath the kitchen window.

"Clara, you've got to calm down," Dad said. "We don't know what's going on."

A chair scraped against the floor.

"I have a bad feeling about that man," Mom cried. "I can't explain it."

Two long rings of the phone filled the kitchen. Mr. Brock's ring tone. A cup clattered to the countertop.

"Don't pick up the phone," Dad said.

"I have to know what's going on," Mom pleaded.

Emily stood on her tippy toes but couldn't reach the window to see inside. Her heart thumped wildly. She strained to hear something, anything.

"Clara?" Dad asked.

"It's about Paul," Mom answered, her voice cracking. "He's missing in action."

Emily slid to the ground. Missing in action? What did that mean? She pulled her knees to her chest as tight as she could and then squeezed even tighter. Paul was Greg's closest friend, and her friend. He was family. Was Paul still in

Vietnam? If Paul was missing, would he be found?

The last time she'd seen him was over a year ago. He'd picked her up and plopped her in a wheelbarrow. Greg and Paul had taken turns pushing her around the yard. She'd been afraid of tumbling from the wheelbarrow as it wobbled and bumped across the grass. Those boys had laughed until they couldn't push her any longer. It hadn't been funny at the time. But now, Emily would gladly get back in the wheelbarrow. She wanted to hear them laugh.

The floorboards squeaked in the kitchen. She heard Mom sniffling and clearing her throat. "The man we saw in the car delivered a telegram. Winston had to learn about Paul from a telegram!"

"Look at me," Dad said. "Look at me. This doesn't mean Greg is in danger."

Emily couldn't wait another second. She rushed to the steps, took them two at a time, and burst into the kitchen.

"Is Greg missing? Where is Paul? Where is Greg?"

"Whoa now, Emily. Slow down." Dad pulled her into his arms.

Emily gulped air as she breathed into Dad's shirt. "I heard you talking. Is that why we haven't had any letters from

Greg?"

"He's not missing," Dad said.

Mom pulled a tissue from her pocket and dabbed at her eyes. She handed some to Dad and Emily.

Emily took a deep breath, and asked, "But Paul is missing. What does that mean?"

Dad wiped his nose and leaned against the table. "It means Paul is not with his fellow soldiers."

"Where is he?" Emily asked. "Can't his friends find him?"

"The military is trying to find him, but it's not an easy thing to do," he responded.

"Then let's tell someone that Greg will find Paul," Emily insisted. "I know he will."

"I wish it were that easy," Mom said. She just stood there, like a statue. Emily didn't know what to say to her, and she still didn't understand why no one could find Paul.

At the sound of Grandpa's truck, Dad hurried outside.

"I need some time alone," Mom said. She rubbed her forehead. "I'm going to lie down for a bit."

Emily moved to the screen door and watched Grandpa get

out of his truck. When Dad embraced him, she wanted to run to them, but held back. Instead, she stepped outside and sat on the steps. She heard bits and pieces of their conversation, a telegram, a mission, and a search. And then Dad and Grandpa headed off toward the orchard. Right then, Emily knew there was more to this story. She also knew where to find the facts.

She wheeled her bike from the garage, jumped on and headed straight to Mr. Brock's farm. Emily slowed as she rode up her neighbor's driveway. Four cars were parked near the house. Voices drifted out the windows. Suddenly, it felt wrong to be there. Emily turned onto the grass and rode past the garden. When she reached the chicken coop, she threw down her bike and opened the sagging door. The puppies ran to her. Emily bent over and scooped up as many puppies as she could hold and snuggled them.

Lilyanne nosed her pockets, and Emily realized she'd left the bacon at the restaurant. She ran her hands along Lilyanne's sides. "Looks like you're starving."

As Emily searched for dog food in the big barn Lilyanne followed and the pups followed their mother. Emily finally found a partial bag of food with a bowl inside. She scooped two handfuls of nuggets and put them in the bowl. Lilyanne gulped down the food in seconds. Her pups wanted some, but she growled at them.

"Poor puppies," Emily said. "Don't mind your momma. She's hungry. You must be, too."

Next, she hurried to the well pump and filled the pail half full. Water sloshed everywhere, mainly into her shoes. "Not again!" she groaned, as she made her way to the chicken coop.

She added water and nuggets to a bowl, stirring until the food turned into mush. The pups devoured it. She mixed up another bowl, and another, until all the pups were fed. Lilyanne finished the leftovers and licked her pups clean. Emily stepped out of the coop, secured the door, and sat cross-legged in the grass. The pups ran around, wrestled and nipped each other until they grew tired and piled on top of each other. All was good in her puppy world.

A few minutes later Grandpa showed up. "I thought you'd be here. How are the pups?"

"They're good, "Emily said.

"Did you feed Sir Taylor, Knight and Dandy Lady?"

Emily jumped up. "I forgot about them."

"Then we'd better do that next."

After cleaning the chicken coop, Emily and Grandpa walked over to the hunting dogs. The dogs barked and leaped against the chicken wire fence. Emily still felt bad for them, and vowed to never have a dog in a cage.

Grandpa cleaned the kennel while Emily took Dandy Lady for a walk. Sir Taylor was next, and then Knight. After their walks, she helped Grandpa feed the dogs and refresh their water.

"Break time," Grandpa said.

He headed toward the well pump while Emily sat near the dogs. Caring for all of them was hard work, but she felt good doing it.

Grandpa returned a quart jar of cold water.

"I'm scared Mr. Brock won't take care of the puppies, or his dogs," Emily said. "Maybe we should come every day to take care of them."

Grandpa took a big drink and passed the jar to Emily. "Good idea. Mr. Brock is plenty worried over Paul right now. I'll let him know we want to help."

Emily's breath caught in her throat. She hadn't thought about Paul, or Greg, the whole time she'd been caring for the dogs, and that made her feel bad. She scrunched her face, wrestling with her feelings.

Grandpa gave her a nudge. "What's on your mind?"

What question should she ask first? She had so many. "Dad said missing in action means Paul isn't with his friends. How could he go missing?"

"Things happen in a war that can't be explained. Think on it this way, Emmy. Somehow Paul got separated from his friends and right now they haven't found him. But they will. They won't give up."

Emily grabbed his hand. "Is Greg missing, too? We haven't heard from him in a long time."

"Absolutely not," Grandpa said. "He isn't MIA. The military would know, and they'd let us know." He put his hand over his heart and patted his chest. "Greg isn't missing. So, get rid of that notion right now."

"Is he really coming home soon?"

Grandpa rose and helped her to her feet. "Very soon. You go on home now. I'll be along shortly. I'll let Winston know we'll take care of all his dogs."

Emily said goodbye to the puppies and their momma. She rode her bike toward the road. She saw some cars leaving, yet more were arriving. Mr. Brock sure was getting a lot of company.

***

During dinner the phone rang off the hook. Every time it rang Emily stopped eating. It was hard to ignore because two long rings meant the calls were for Mr. Brock.

"Truck will be ready tomorrow," Dad said. "It's back to work for me. I'll be on the road most of the week and probably late for dinner every night."

Grandpa cleared his throat. "Emily and I want to team up and take care of Winston's dogs. I ran the idea past him and he's agreeable if it's okay with the two of you." He looked at Mom and Dad. "I thought we'd go there each day after school."

Mom nodded. "As long as Emily keeps up on her homework, and doesn't get attached to those pups, it's fine with me."

"Agreed," Dad said. "How's Winston holding up?"

"As well as can be expected," Grandpa answered.

The phone rang again. On the fourth short ring, Emily rushed to answer it.

"Hello," a woman said. "I saw a poster today about some puppies for sale. I'd like to know what color they are."

Emily had been so busy with Mr. Brock's dogs and the puppies that she'd forgotten about the posters. "They're all different colors," she answered quickly.

"Is one of them yellow or golden brown?"

"Yes," Emily said. "Her name is Goldie."

"And how much are you asking for Goldie?"

"Um, two dollars."

"Thank you. I'll call back if interested. Goodbye."

Emily shuffled back to the table.

"Well?" Mom asked.

"The lady said she'd call back if interested."

After that, everyone was quiet. Too quiet. Were they thinking about the puppies, or about Paul or Greg, or both? Emily had to end the awkward silence.

"I promise to do my best with Mr. Brock's dogs. I'll help take care of them, so Mr. Brock doesn't have to worry. And I'm going to work hard to sell the puppies, so that everyone of them finds a good home."

"That's a good plan," Dad said.

Grandpa winked at Emily and gave her a big smile.

"It sounds like something my *Emily* would do," Mom said, and for the first time since the news about Paul, Emily saw Mom's smile reach her eyes.

And in that moment, Emily didn't feel so powerless.

CHAPTER 10

Show and Tell

The next morning, Mom drove her to school. Emily was going to show the last poster to her classmates during Show and Tell. She'd written each puppy's name on the poster in alphabetical order. She couldn't wait to share stories about them with her classmates.

In the hallway, before classes started, some of the kids were talking about Paul Brock being missing-in-action. Some of the boys said Paul might have been killed. KIA, they called it. Hearing those words made Emily's stomach knot up. If Paul was KIA, then Greg might be KIA. She felt like she was going to throw up and was sent to the school nurse.

Miss Swinson checked Emily for a fever. She checked her

eyes, nose and throat. "You seem to be fine, so tell me what's made you upset today," she asked.

"Nothing."

"Well, I think I know what's wrong. Look at me, Emily."

She looked.

"Paul will be found. You keep on believing that. One day soon, those boys will both be home. And you'll be glad you didn't waste a single minute fretting over them."

"How do you know for sure?" Emily asked.

"I believe it, and you should, too. And right now, you have school and studies to focus on. Okay?"

Emily couldn't answer. She wasn't okay. She still felt sick.

"Back to class you go," Miss Swinson said. "Come and see me later today if you're still feeling the same."

Show and Tell was in progress when Emily entered her classroom. She slid into her assigned seat. Listening to the kids share their weekend activities helped Emily get her mind away from her worries. When it was her turn, she carried her poster to the front of the room. She reminded herself that finding homes for the puppies was something important she could do to help Mr. Brock.

"Lilyanne is my neighbor's hunting dog and she has ten puppies. Their names are Brownie, Bruiser, Caramel, Goldie, Henry, Pumpkin, Rusty, Sandy, Sarah and Splotches." She put her finger on each name as she read them to the class. "They're the cutest puppies and lots of fun to play with. But they need new homes. I hope you'll want to buy one."

John raised his hand, and Mrs. Bayne called on him.

"Why don't you give them away?" he asked.

Emily paused. "My neighbor doesn't want to do that. I'm helping find them good homes." She wanted to blab the whole story about how she'd rescued the puppies and took them to her farm, but Mom had made her promise not to bring it up.

"Do you have anything more to tell us?" Mrs. Bayne asked.

John raised his hand again. "What will happen if they don't find homes?"

Emily hesitated. *What would happen? Mr. Brock said he'd keep the pups. But would he?* She felt sick again, stared at the floor and bit her lip.

"Emily?" Mrs. Bayne called her name. "Are you all right?"

"Let me know if you want a puppy. Thank you," Emily

said. She rushed to her seat.

Lunch followed Show and Tell, but Emily wasn't hungry.

"Earth to Emily."

Emily looked up to see her cousin standing in the doorway to her classroom.

"Are you coming to lunch?" Sarah asked.

Most of the class had already cleared out. Mrs. Bayne stood at the front of the room, waiting for Emily to leave.

"Everything is going to be okay," her teacher said with a smile. "I hope you find homes for all those puppies."

"Puppies?" Sarah asked. "What puppies?"

Emily remembered that Sarah didn't know what happened over the weekend. She dashed to the door, grabbed Sarah's hand, and the two headed to the cafeteria. Once seated and eating lunch, she told her cousin the whole rescue story.

"You did that all by yourself?" Sarah's eyes got big.

Emily nodded. "I called to tell you about the puppies, but you were at your dads."

"I wish I'd been home," Sarah said. She pulled a sandwich from her paper sack. "Weren't you scared taking the puppies to your farm?"

Emily shook her head. "I just had to do it. I had to save the puppies."

"You're brave, Emily. The puppies are lucky to have you as their friend."

Emily smiled. "Thanks!"

***

After lunch with Sarah, Emily felt a lot better. By the end of the day Emily believed she would find homes for the pups. Several kids and two teachers had shown interest. Her good feelings left, though, when she climbed on the bus. Because of the seat squashing she'd received on Friday from the Trenton sisters, she'd rather walk home.

She plopped into her assigned seat. Karen Thomas, in the seat ahead of her, turned. "I heard about the puppies you're selling. That's neat."

"Thank you," Emily said.

"I'm going to ask my parents if we can get one."

"Really?" Emily said. "I'll have the puppies at my house this weekend and you could stop by and see them."

"Sure," Karen said. "I'd like to."

A few minutes later, Sissy and Carol boarded the bus.

"I'm sitting by the window today," Sissy ordered Emily, forcing her way past Emily. Carol shoved up against Emily and sat with her legs in the aisle.

"I need more room," Carol ordered. She pushed against Emily which made Emily smash against Sissy.

"Get off me," Sissy growled.

"I can't," Emily said, squirming. "Carol's on me."

Sissy reached across Emily and slugged her sister's arm. "Move over. Now!"

"Don't tell me what to do," Carol growled. Sissy shook her fist at her sister.

Emily gulped and stared straight ahead not wanting to get in between their battle. But she was in the middle, whether she liked it or not.

"Wait until we get home and I tell Mom," Carol said with a sneer.

Sissy shrugged. "Go ahead and tell. She'll believe me before she believes you."

Carol, for once, didn't respond.

Emily was speechless. And then she noticed kids around them had been watching the argument. She looked at the mirror over Mr. Allen's head. He'd seen it, too. Not good. Not good at all. She sat there as quietly as possible as the bus left the school and headed toward the safety of her home.

When the sisters got off at their house, Emily took a deep breath. She was thankful they'd left her alone. Those girls were a giant puzzle; one she couldn't piece together.

The bus pulled up to her driveway. Emily dashed off without even a goodbye to Mr. Allen. She didn't want to talk to anyone right then. She checked their mailbox, found it empty, and ran for home.

"Mom!" Emily yelled as she entered the house. "Did anyone call for a puppy?"

"No phone calls," Mom said as she entered the kitchen. "But something else happened."

"What?" Emily grumped. What could be more important than the puppies?

Mom brought her hand from behind her back.

Emily saw letters, lots and lots of letters!

CHAPTER 11

Letters from Greg

Mom spread the letters on the table while Emily jumped around the room, whooping and hollering.

"Three are for you," Mom said.

Emily scanned the table. Right away she noticed an envelope with her name on it. She quickly found the other two and clutched them to her chest.

"Can I read them now? Can I?"

"Of course. When you're done, will you read them to me?"

"I will, Mom, I will."

Emily dashed outside to the front porch and plopped down on the steps. She tore open the first envelope. It was dated August 25.

Hi Em,

I'm thinking about you every day. I've been wondering how you're doing since school has started again. What's your favorite class? Are you working on any projects yet?

I have a nature fact for you. There are 8-10" centipedes here, in different colors. Some have bright yellow legs. All have sharp claws. They curl up next to us when we sleep on the ground and we don't know they're there. We hope we don't roll over on them because they pinch, and it hurts. OUCH, OUCH, OUCH. Don't worry. I haven't slept on one yet. Other guys have, and it's not good.

Centipedes? Emily stuck out her tongue. She hated bugs.

The country is pretty, but the mountains are beautiful. We're still on the move and only make it to base camp every few weeks. I received four letters from you last week. I'm glad you're writing to me. Arm pinch for good luck.

Love, Greg

She tore open the other two envelopes. Both letters were short and written on scrap paper.

August 12

Hey Sis,

I hope you still love to draw because you're good at it. Send me a drawing and I'll carry it with me. I've been thinking about your problem with Carol and Sissy. Grandpa told me their dad went away to find work. The girls must miss him very much. I'm sure they don't understand why he's been gone for so long. My advice is the same: be nice to them. Once they know their words aren't bothering you, they should leave you alone. Bullies keep on bullying when they get a reaction. So, give it a try, sis. Be EXTRA nice and let me know how it works out.

I've got to go now. I'm out on a mission. Hold this letter close to your heart because it contains a GREAT BIG HUG.

Love, Greg

The next letter was even shorter.

August 8

To my silly sister,

I'm going to ask a big favor. Please give Mom twenty hugs from me because she's missing me (I can tell from her letters). Give Grandpa ten. But Dad only gets five because that's probably all he'll let you give him. Don't forget to hug Queenie, too.

Love, your brother

Emily's heart thumped. She couldn't give Queenie hugs. But she could hug Mom and Dad and Grandpa.

She gathered her letters and envelopes and went inside. Mom sat at the kitchen table, stirring her coffee, but otherwise not moving. Some letters had been opened and were face down on the table. Others were unopened and stacked in a pile.

"Aren't you going to read them?" Emily asked.

Mom put her hand on her chest. "Goodness, I was lost in thought. What did you say, dear?"

"Are you going to read the letters?"

"Oh, yes. When your father gets home," she said. She patted the chair next to her. "What news did your brother send?"

Emily slid into the chair, unfolded the two short letters and read them. After that, she leaned over and hugged Mom. "I owe you nineteen more from Greg. I think I'll give you a couple of them a day and not use them all up at once."

With tears in her eyes Mom laughed, and Emily did, too.

"And guess what! I've already made him a picture of the puppies!"

"He will love it," Mom said. "Now, what about the other letter?"

Emily began reading but stopped when she heard a truck rumble up the driveway.

"Dad's home!" She ran out to meet him. "Dad! Greg sent fourteen letters. Three are for me."

Her father scooped her up and twirled her around. "Fourteen is a lot of letters." He put Emily back on her feet and said, "We'll be celebrating tonight."

Emily couldn't let go. Not yet. She hugged Dad as hard as she could. "That's from Greg."

Dad held her for a long time. "You've made my day."

After dinner, they remained at the kitchen table. Mom had

stacked the letters in front of her and kept running her fingers along their edges.

"Well, are we reading them or looking at them," Grandpa asked.

"Reading!" Dad said. "Let's get started."

The letters were written at different times. Some had arrived quickly; others had been delayed. The last time they'd received mail from Greg was the first week of August, and it was now the middle of September.

Greg referred to himself and other soldiers as grunts. He wrote about the heat and humidity, and the rain as the monsoon season was still going on. Only once did he mention bugs, and that was in Emily's letter. Greg also wrote he was at LZ Donna and he might be there for a while. Emily remembered from previous letters that LZs were landing zones where base camps were set up.

In almost every letter Greg asked for more stationery. He wrote that it was hard to keep paper dry due to the weather, and when he found time to write the paper was usually ruined.

A couple of times when Mom or Dad read a letter, they'd pause briefly before continuing. The same thing had happened in the past, and it always left Emily wondering what her parents were keeping to themselves.

"Greg still asks about Queenie," Grandpa said. "I feel bad he doesn't know she died. I hope we did the right thing by not telling him."

"Me, too, Henry," Mom said.

"I believe we did," Dad said. "It's better to tell him face-to-face."

Silence followed until Mom brought over a plate of cookies from the counter and set it on the table.

"How was your day, Emily?" she asked.

"Pretty good. I showed the kids in my class the puppy poster. Some said they'd ask their parents if they could buy one."

Mom put her hand over Emily's hand. "That's a good start in getting the news out about the puppies." She rose and picked up the plates. "Help me in the kitchen before you do your homework."

Dad and Grandpa went outside. Emily cleared the table while Mom washed dishes. Afterward, she went to her room and studied for a spelling test. She had some arithmetic worksheets to complete, too. An hour later, Mom brought her a glass of water.

"How's it going?"

"I finished my homework," Emily said. "Will you ask me my spelling words?"

"Sure." Mom sat on the bed and recited the words while Emily spelled them verbally.

"A+," Mom said. "Good job. Now, I've got something important to ask you. Your dad and I think it's best if we don't mention Greg's letters to other people. It's because of what's happening right now with Paul. If people find out we've received letters from Greg they are likely to ask Mr. Brock about Paul. We don't want to cause Mr. Brock any further pain. Does that make sense?"

Emily nodded. "But I have to tell Sarah about Greg. She'll be upset if I don't."

"I'm sure Aunt Chris has told her," Mom answered. "They're coming over tomorrow night. Now, get some sleep. See you in the morning."

As she laid in bed, waiting to fall asleep, Emily made a list of things to do when Sarah came over. Now that she knew Greg was okay and would be home soon, she could focus her attention on the puppies. And the first item on her agenda was to take her cousin to see them. Sarah was going to love them as much as she did.

Before drifting off to sleep, Emily said a quick prayer, thankful that the end of her day turned out so much better than the beginning.

CHAPTER 12

Cousins and Puppies

On Tuesday evening, Emily twirled in the tire swing while she waited for Aunt Chris and Sarah to arrive. A couple of minutes later, their station wagon came up the driveway.

"Mom! They're here," Emily yelled. She untangled from the swing and ran to meet them. Sarah jumped out and they grabbed each other's hands.

"I'm so happy to see you," her cousin said. "I have so much to share."

"I do, too," Emily exclaimed.

Aunt Chris gave her a kiss on the cheek. "It's good to see you, Emily. It's been too long since we were together. Is your mom cooking up a storm?"

"Of course!" Emily said.

"Then I'd better get inside and help her." Aunt Chris headed to the house.

"We have the whole night together," Sarah said. "What are we going to do first?"

"Go see the puppies!" Emily said.

The girls linked arms and ran to the house. Mom gave them the okay to ride to Mr. Brock's. "But be back by six-thirty for dinner."

They pulled Sarah's bike out of the station wagon and Emily got hers from the garage. Hopping on, the girls raced to Mr. Brock's farm. At the chicken coop, Emily slid to a stop.

"Here they are!"

The pups were piled up at the coop door as they dropped their bikes. Ten yipping, yapping, tail-shaking puppies, and Lilyanne. Emily opened the door and the pups piled out. Sarah clapped her hands, laughing. She bent down and touched as many pups as she could reach.

Emily lifted one up. "This one has your name."

Sarah took the pup in her arms and nuzzled her. "You are

so sweet."

"They follow each other like cars in a train," Emily said. "Come on, I'll show you."

The girls led the puppy train out of the coop and to the lawn. From there, the pups headed in every direction while their mother rolled around, scratching her back. The pups chased each other. Emily and Sarah threw sticks for them.

"Want to see where I found them the first time?" Emily asked.

"Sure," Sarah replied.

They put the pups back in the coop, but Lilyanne didn't want to go in.

"You need some exercise, don't you, girl," Emily said. "She can come with us."

The girls raced around the barn and stopped for a few minutes to pet the hunting dogs.

"This is Knight, Dandy Lady and Sir Taylor," Emily said, pointing to each dog.

"Do they ever get out to play?" Sarah asked.

Emily shook her head. "But Grandpa and I feed and exercise them. He says I can't let them out because they're not my dogs. I got in enough trouble when I took Lilyanne and the pups to my house."

The girls stuck their fingers through the wire fencing and scratched the dogs' noses.

"Catch me if you can!" Emily took off running again. She sprinted down the dirt road toward the creepy old shed where she'd found the puppies. Lilyanne kept pace beside her.

Sarah caught up and punched Emily's arm. "Tag, you're it. Why'd you stop?"

"This is where Lilyanne hid her pups." Emily pointed to the shed.

Sarah scrunched her face. "In there?"

Emily nodded. "It's not so bad inside," she said, giggling. "Want to go in?"

Sarah held up her hands and backed away. "Nope. I don't." She crossed her arms and frowned. "But I wish I had been here to help with your rescue."

"Me, too," Emily answered. She heard the dinner bell ringing in the distance. "Uh oh. We've got to go."

Several minutes later, after putting Lilyanne back with the puppies, they tumbled into the kitchen, shoving and laughing.

"Wash up, girls. The food is almost ready," Emily's mom said. "It's just us for dinner. Dad and Grandpa should be here in time for dessert."

The girls washed and took a seat at the dining room table. Warm bread, crisp pickles and a fruit salad filled the table's center. Aunt Chris brought over pork chops and green beans. Emily's mom carried a bowl of mashed potatoes. After they said grace, they passed the food dishes around. Emily took heaping amounts of everything, and so did Sarah.

Mom and Aunt Chris chatted without stopping. Emily noticed they barely touched their food. Suddenly, Emily's mom stood and pushed back her chair. She motioned for Aunt Chris to go with her.

"We'll be right back," Aunt Chris said. "Finish up without us."

"What's going on?" Sarah asked.

"I don't know," Emily said, "but they're acting really strange."

A few minutes later, Emily went down the hall to the bathroom. When she passed her parent's bedroom, she saw her mom and Aunt Chris inside. Emily pressed against the wall and listened as Aunt Chris talked.

"You've got to stop reading that letter, Clara. It does you no good to keep worrying. Sounds to me like Greg needed to share his heart with someone he loves."

"I know, I know." Mom sniffed.

"Now blow your nose and let's get you freshened up," Aunt Chris said. "You're a mess."

Emily ducked into the bathroom and shut the door. *What were they talking about?* The door handles wiggled.

"I'm in here," Emily said.

"Let's go upstairs," Aunt Chris said.

Emily sat on the edge of the bathtub and remembered the day Greg's letters arrived. Mom had opened a couple of them, but said she'd wanted to read the rest when Dad got home. It must have been the first time she'd read about whatever was worrying her.

She returned to the table just as Mom and Aunt Chris came back. Mom's face showed telltale signs of crying, but she was trying to act as though nothing happened.

Aunt Chris picked up her purse and casserole dish. "Well, I hate to end this evening, but we really must be going. After all, there is school tomorrow. We had a great time, and we're looking forward to the day when Greg comes home."

"But Mom, I don't want to go yet," Sarah said.

Aunt Chris gave her "the look" and Sarah got up. And then they were gone, lickety split.

"Why'd they have to go so soon?" Emily asked.

"It's complicated," Mom answered. "Let's clean up. It seems we've all missed dessert tonight."

Emily tried not to be worried about Mom's behavior, but she still had lots of questions. There was so much more she'd wanted to do with Sarah. She hadn't even shared Greg's letters with her.

Later, as Emily lay in bed reading, she heard a knock on the door.

"Can I turn out your light?" Mom asked, peeking into the room.

Emily shook her head. "Not yet. I have a question."

"What, honey?"

"I heard you crying earlier," Emily said.

"Oh, your Aunt Chris didn't mean to make me cry. Some days are harder for me than others."

"And that's all?"

Mom flipped off the light switch. "All is well so sleep

tight. Today is done and tomorrow will be what it will be."

Lying in the darkness, Emily knew Mom hadn't told the truth. Well, not the whole truth. She rolled on her side, closed her eyes and knew she had to find that letter.

CHAPTER 13

A Letter to Find

The next morning, Emily woke to an angry rain pelting the house. She snuggled deeper under the covers. Suddenly, her bedroom door flew open and the light came on.

"Get up!" Mom said. "You're going to be late for the bus."

Emily slid out of bed, dressed as fast as she could and brushed her teeth. She gathered her homework and dashed down the stairs.

"Let's get a move on," Mom said. "You'll need your raincoat and boots. Here's your lunch."

Emily took the sack and noticed something sticking out of Mom's sleeve. It looked like the corner of a letter. Before she could ask about it, Mom grabbed her keys and headed out the door. Emily quickly followed.

"I can't believe I fell back asleep after your father left," Mom said as she drove down the driveway. "I don't like being rushed in the morning."

"Me either," Emily said. She still wasn't fully awake and yawned long and loud.

Mom slowed the car and parked at the end of their driveway. "Oh, good. There's Mr. Allen. Have a great day, sweetie."

"Thanks Mom," Emily said as she got out and dashed to the bus. By the time she climbed the steps, though, her pants were soaked. She slid into her seat and the bus roared to life.

Lightning flashed and thunder rumbled. Emily's thoughts immediately went to the puppies and Lilyanne. She hoped they were safe and dry inside the chicken coop house. She would check on them after school.

Three stops later the Trenton sisters climbed aboard. Mr. Allen said something to them before they passed him, and the girls jostled down the aisle. Emily dreaded the moment they'd all be smashed together in the same soaked seat. But instead of pushing into her seat, the girls passed by with only a glare from Carol.

When the bus started to move again, Emily glanced over her shoulder and saw them sitting three rows back. Quickly, she turned and faced the front of the bus. *Mr. Allen must have told them to sit there. But why?* She tried not to worry, but thoughts of future bullying filled her head. Emily made sure she was one of the first kids off the bus.

***

During the morning recess, their teacher kept them inside and busy with a writing assignment. Emily received a list of words and she had to think about other words that rhymed. She had fun with the assignment.

Art class replaced their afternoon recess. Mrs. Bayne let them choose what to make. Emily decided to draw a picture of Queenie. She didn't want to forget what she looked like. It wasn't the best thing she'd drawn, but it did resemble Queenie. After art, the rest of the school day plodded by, rainy and gloomy. Emily slumped in her chair and counted the hours until she would see Lilyanne and the pups again. It seemed like forever.

A break in the weather gave Emily time to board the bus without getting wet. She piled her books on her lap and waited for the usual seatmate trouble.

Sissy Trenton came down the aisle, but Carol wasn't with her. Sissy slid next to Emily and sat there quietly instead of demanding to sit by the window. Emily didn't say anything, and neither did Sissy. The silence between them grew thicker by the second.

When the bus screeched to a stop at the Trenton's house, Sissy whispered, "I hope you find homes for the puppies." And then she hurried off the bus.

Emily's books almost slid off her lap. *Sissy was nice? It had to be a mistake. Was it because her sister wasn't there?* No matter why, it made Emily feel good if only this one time.

At her stop, Emily rushed off the bus. "Bye Mr. Allen."

She couldn't wait to change her clothes and go see the puppies. Inside the mudroom, she tossed off her coat and boots, and set her shoes and books on a chair.

"Hi, sweetie," Mom said as Emily entered the kitchen. "How was your day?"

"Pretty good," Emily said. "We had art class in the afternoon because we couldn't go out for recess."

"Oh? And what did you make?" Mom asked.

"I drew a picture of Queenie, but I left it at school so it wouldn't get rained on."

"Well, I can't wait to see it," Mom said.

"Where's Grandpa? It's time to go to Mr. Brock's."

Mom rustled through the cupboards, clanging pots and pans. "He's there now. He said not to worry about helping him today."

Emily rushed to put on her boots.

"Where do you think you're going?" Mom asked.

"Grandpa should have waited for me. We're a team."

"You are not going anywhere. Look outside. It's pouring again."

Abruptly, Emily melted into her own little puddle of tears.

Mom knelt beside her. "What's wrong?"

Emily wiped her eyes with the bottom of her shirt. "I have to go. The puppies are my responsibility! I can't do anything about Greg, or Paul, but I can help the puppies!" She released her frustrations and the bottled-up worry into new tears.

"Grandpa didn't wait because he hoped to finish cutting the grass before it rained."

Emily closed her eyes and leaned against the wall.

"Sweetie, Grandpa will feel awful if he thinks you're mad at him."

"I'm not mad!"

Mom held Emily's hands. "Tell me what's bothering you."

"I don't know," Emily said. "I feel all itchy inside, like something bad is going to happen. Or something bad has already happened, and I don't know about it."

"We can't wait on bad news, Emily. If it comes, it comes," Mom said, helping Emily to her feet. "I've got an idea. Let's make Grandma's oatmeal cookies to keep your mind off 'itchy' things."

In the bathroom, Emily blew her nose and washed her hands. She didn't feel like making cookies. She still felt guilty because she wasn't helping with the dogs. She looked forward to helping. It was the best part of her day.

"Come on," Mom called. "Let's get going on the cookies."

Emily mixed the dry ingredients, while Mom beat the sugar and shortening, then added eggs and vanilla. When the dough was ready, they placed tablespoons of it on the cookie sheet. After that, the cookies went into the oven.

Emily took a break and walked into the dining room. She saw a stack of letters on the table. When she picked them up and read the envelopes, she noticed they were for Mr. Brock. And they were all from Paul. Emily sniffed the envelopes. They had an earthy smell, like garden dirt. She ran her hands over them, and somehow felt closer to Paul. *I hope you're safe, Paul, wherever you are.*

Mom came into the room, wiping her hands with a towel.

"Why do we have Mr. Brock's letters?" Emily asked.

Mom took them and placed them back on the table. "Winston is visiting his sister for a couple of days, and Grandpa is collecting his mail until he returns."

Emily was puzzled. "But how could he leave now with Paul missing?"

"I think the phone calls and visitors got to be too much for him," Mom answered. "He's had a lot going on and needs rest to heal his leg. It's good for his sister to take care of him."

"What if Paul comes home and nobody's there?"

"If that were to happen, I think Paul would come here."

Emily nodded. "He would. He'd come here right away."

"That's right," Mom said. "So, while Mr. Brock is gone, we'll collect his mail and keep the letters safe for his return."

Emily saw Mom reach into her apron pocket; she'd seen

her do it earlier when baking cookies. She believed a letter was in the apron, and it was the one that made Mom cry. She had to find a way to get it.

The wind-up oven timer rang, and Mom hurried into the kitchen. The kitchen smelled sweet and sugary. While those cookies cooled, another tray went into the oven and an hour later they had six dozen cookies cooling on the counter.

Emily went to her room and tackled her homework. When she finished, she thought again about Grandpa and how she hadn't been there to help with Mr. Brock's dogs. She hoped he would stop by and give her an update on the puppies.

She went back downstairs to get a drink of water. Mom stood in the hallway with her back to the stairs. She held the phone to her ear, but she wasn't talking. *Oh no! Mom was listening in on someone else's call.* And it wasn't the first time. Since hearing about Paul, Mom had often listened in on party line calls.

Emily scooted around the corner and went through the utility room to the kitchen. She got a glass from the cupboard, filled it with water, and backed out of the kitchen. As she did, she saw Mom's apron hanging on a hook next to the window. She stopped, glancing around to make sure she wasn't seen, and searched the pockets. She felt the edge of an envelope and pulled it out. It was from Greg.

This is it, she thought. It must be the letter that made Mom cry.

CHAPTER 14

Words from War

Emily pressed the letter to her chest and hurried to her room. She sat on the floor with her back against the bed. She took a deep breath and slowly pulled the paper from the envelope. Smoothing it flat against her leg, Emily saw Greg's handwriting and began to read:

> *August 17*
>
> *Mom and Dad,*
>
> *I'm sad. So sad. Heartbroken. I know it's not fair of me to share this with you because you worry enough already, but I'll explode if I don't release some feelings. This war is awful. No, it's HORRIBLE.*

Every day we wonder if we're going to make it through alive. There are things I'll never be able to tell you, because – well, I can't. But I need to talk to you because two of my best friends, Jack O'Brien, Jack-O we call him, and Ben "Beanie" Brown, were critically injured this week. Gosh, it's hard to talk about them in a letter, but harder on me if I don't. All the guys are close in some way, but Jack-O and Beanie and I are close. Like Paul and me. I'm not going to tell you the details, but I was <u>RIGHT THERE</u> when it happened. I wanted to put down my gun and run to them, but I couldn't. I had to keep fighting. I yelled for the medics until they reached Jack-O and Beanie. I'm so upset I can't see straight. They were the same age as me and too young to have this happen!

The tears from earlier threatened to come back. Emily never imagined any of this. She'd always thought of the war as an adventure for her brother, and that he wasn't in danger. Well, she had believed it until Paul became MIA, and then she'd started worrying that Greg could also be MIA.

But all this time he'd been in danger. All this time he

could have been injured or killed. But he wasn't. He was alive, and he was hurting. Emily rubbed her eyes until she could see clearly and read some more:

> *I almost didn't send this letter. I put it away for a day to give it some more thought. I'm sending it because I need your prayers now more than ever. For Jack-O and Beanie and their families. These are hard times for everyone involved in this war.*
>
> *Until I come home, I'm sending my love to you, to Grandpa and Emily. Stay strong for me. That's what I need right now.*
>
> *Love, Greg*

Emily put the letter on the floor, pulled her knees to her chest and bawled. Nothing would be the same now that she knew the truth. Nothing.

Her mind went back to letters Greg had sent her. He'd never said a bad word about the war, or the country, or the people. He'd only told her funny stuff, and icky bug stuff. His letters had been filled with silly facts and interesting information. His letters always made her happy.

Rain beat down on the roof, louder and louder. Emily

crumpled the letter in her fist. She couldn't bear to be alone. She flew down the stairs and into her mother's arms.

Mom held her tight, then looked into Emily's eyes. "What's wrong? Please tell me."

"I know Greg's in danger."

"What?" Mom asked. "I don't understand."

Emily held out the crumpled letter. "I found this in your apron."

At first Mom looked shocked, but then her face softened. She took the letter and laid it on the table.

"I had to know why you were sad," she said. "But now I'm sorry I read it."

"Come with me." Mom took Emily's hand and led her to the living room sofa.

"I'm sorry. I never meant for you learn about the war this way," Mom said. "I should have told you more, because you wanted to know more. I realize that now."

"Families don't keep secrets," Emily said, her voice shaking.

"We're not keeping secrets. We're trying to protect you from unpleasant things," Mom explained. "Like how we were protecting Greg, by not telling him about Queenie."

"But he's in danger. His friends were injured, Mom. He could be injured, or even killed. Why can't he come home right now?"

"He can't come home until he's served his time," she said." And I'll bet he's as anxious to get home as we are to have him get here. Until we know more, we need to be patient. And we can pray. Pray for his safe return."

"It's hard," Emily said. "Even harder knowing Greg's in danger."

Mom sighed. "You're right. It is harder now than it was before. But we'll get through it. Now give me one of those hugs he promised me."

Emily did just that.

"We can discuss this again anytime you want." Mom got to her feet. "But right now, I'm going to spend some time praying for those boys and their families."

"Jack-O and Beanie," Emily said.

"Yes, Jack-O and Beanie." Mom nodded. "Thank you for reminding me of their names."

Emily returned to her room. She pulled out paper and a pencil and began to write. The words spilled from her heart faster than she could put them to the page. She stopped twice and rewrote her sentences. The letter had to be perfect. At last she finished and read it over.

Hi Greg,

I miss you so much. Lots of things are happening here. Remember I said I rescued the puppies? I told Mr. Brock I would find good homes for them. We made a deal. I get the puppies this weekend and I'm supposed to sell them for $2.00 each. I made posters and we put them around town. The pups are so cute. You'd love them. Their names are Caramel, Sarah, Henry, Rusty, Brownie, Bruiser, Sandy, Goldie, Splotches and Pumpkin. Pumpkin is my favorite and I want to keep her. I hope I can. Grandpa and I are a team. Every day we take care of the puppies, and Lilyanne, Sir Taylor, Knight, and Dandy Lady. They're lonely without Paul.

I know your friends got hurt bad. I wasn't supposed to read the letter, but Mom and Dad were sad, and I wanted to know why. Now I know the war is horrible. Jack-O and Beanie are nice names. They are my friends now, too. I'll say a prayer every night for their families, and for you and Paul. I think about you all the time. When you are sad you can tell me. And I'll tell you when I'm sad. I'm sad now. Please come home right away. Please! In my next letter I'll tell you if I sold the puppies. But not Pumpkin. I want her to be mine.

Love, Emily

She folded the letter and inserted the puppy picture she'd drawn. Once again, she taped the letter for privacy. She sat there for several minutes, missing Greg. She got on her knees and pulled the hat box from under her bed. She pulled out all the letters from her brother and placed them in a circle around her. And then she began to read.

CHAPTER 15

A Grand Idea

During recess on Friday afternoon, Emily sat on a swing and worried about the puppies. The posters were a big flop. Only three people called during the week, but nobody said for sure they would buy a pup. Emily still hoped they would call back. She would get the puppies tomorrow. And then what? Make more posters? Make bigger posters? If she couldn't find homes for the puppies, they'd go back to Mr. Brock. She could not fail!

Finally, the last bell rang for school dismissal. Emily gathered up her books and papers and dashed to the bus. Grandpa was there, waiting for her.

"Hi Grandpa. What's going on?"

"We're going straight to Mr. Brock's. I need you to take care of the dogs by yourself."

"How come?" Emily asked.

"Winston is still at his sister's, and if I don't finish cutting the grass he won't be able to find his house when he gets back."

Emily laughed. "I can't wait to see the puppies!"

They drove to Mr. Brock's farm and parked next to the big barn. "Let the dogs play in the back yard but keep them away from where I'm mowing. And don't let those pups out."

Emily approached the hunting dogs first. Dandy Lady and Sir Taylor whined for attention. They pushed against the wire fence, begging to be let out. Knight lay there looking quite sad. Emily let the two younger dogs out and they dashed across the yard chasing each other. She entered the kennel and knelt beside Knight.

"Come on, boy. Don't you want to run around? You'll love it in the grass." Slowly, Knight rose and followed her.

After she exercised them, and they were fed and watered, Emily went to see the pups. They yipped and jumped around, demanding her attention, and her heart melted at their cuteness. Lilyanne pawed at the door. Emily opened it slightly, just enough for her to squeeze through. Lilyanne nudged Emily's leg.

"I know you're hungry. Let's find some food."

As the pups and their mother had their dinner, Emily cleaned the coop again. It was a never-ending job, but she was getting faster at doing it. When she finished, she went looking for Grandpa. She found him by the shed, taking a wheel off the mower.

"What happened, Grandpa?"

"It started wobbling. I think I lost a bolt." He tinkered with it a little more, and then stretched. "Looks like I need to buy one from the hardware store. I'll have to finish the grass tomorrow."

"Grandpa, why can't we take the pups home with us right now? I'd have more time with them."

He wiped his hands on a rag. "I can think of two reasons why we shouldn't. First off, we don't have permission."

"But Mr. Brock's not here. He won't miss the puppies."

"And the second reason is Lilyanne is going to miss her pups when they're gone. Are you ready to take them from her?"

Emily thought it over. "I guess Lilyanne would miss

them. But she'll miss them tomorrow, too. Can we take them, please?"

"Are you sure you want to?"

Emily nodded. "As long as we don't get into trouble."

Grandpa laughed. "Don't worry. We won't. I've already talked to Winston and he said we could take the pups whenever we wanted."

"Grandpa! Why didn't you tell me? You sure had me wondering."

"If we take them, we still need to come back here and take care of the hunting dogs."

"I know, and I don't mind," Emily said. "I love the dogs."

"Then let's get those pups."

Grandpa backed the truck up to the barn. He loaded several bales of straw in the truck bed. "We'll use these as a makeshift pen," he explained.

Emily helped Grandpa push the bales to each side of the truck bed to make room for the pups, and then plopped down with a big sigh. "Why don't people want the puppies?"

Grandpa leaned on the tailgate, wiping his brow with handkerchief. "This is a hunting town, Emmy. A mutt might train to be a good hunter. Then again, it might not. Most people don't want to take the chance."

"But $2.00 isn't much to pay for a puppy," Emily said.

"It's enough, and there are other costs involved with having a dog."

"But they're so cute, Grandpa. If people could see them, they'd buy them."

"I agree with you. Still, you'd best prepare yourself in case they don't sell."

Emily couldn't let that happen.

They loaded the pups, and Emily climbed in with them. Lilyanne ran around and around the truck, barking and jumping. It took a little while for Grandpa to catch her. Finally, he grabbed hold of her and put her inside the chicken coop.

As they pulled away, Emily heard Lilyanne's frantic barks. Her stomach lurched, and she covered her ears until they were out of sight. The pups crawled all over her, licking and nipping. Emily would have laughed if she hadn't been sad for Lilyanne.

Back at her house, Emily kept the puppies occupied while Grandpa created a temporary pen for them in the garage.

"Well, what do I see?" Mom called from the porch. "Ten

puppies?"

"Aren't they cute?" Emily ran to her and the pups followed. "Grandpa said we could bring them home today."

Mom picked up a puppy.

"That's Rusty," Emily said.

"Hello, Rusty." Mom put him down and picked up another. "And who is this?

"Goldie." Emily told her their names as Mom met each one.

"They are quite adorable," Mom said. "You'll be a busy bee finding them homes."

Emily picked up Henry and Splotches and whispered, "If people could see you, they would love you."

Suddenly, she had a grand idea.

CHAPTER 16

Come See, Come Buy

The next morning, Emily paced the hallway while her mom called the corner grocery store. She hoped the owner, Mr. Fripp, would let her sell the puppies outside the store. She chewed her fingernails and tried not to interrupt as Mom talked to him.

"All right. That sounds good. Thank you." Mom hung up and broke into a smile.

"What did he say?" Emily asked.

"He said yes! He's happy to help."

Emily twirled around the room. The idea had come to her last night while playing with the puppies. When she'd told her parents, Dad congratulated her on coming up with a great plan.

Emily truly believed if people could see the pups, they couldn't help but buy them.

"When can we go to the store?"

"After lunch. Grandpa will take you. But right now, chores."

Chores! Emily frowned. *Every weekend, chores!*

"Here's your list." Mom handed it to her. "I'm going to town to mail the care package. I won't be long."

Suddenly, a chorus of puppy yips and barks filled the air. Emily dashed outside. Someone had left the side door to the garage open. She found Lilyanne inside, standing in the middle of the puppy pen.

"Hey, girl. You're not supposed to be here." She tugged Lilyanne's neck, but she wouldn't budge.

Mom rushed into the garage. "I heard all the barking. Oh, dear. Lilyanne must miss her pups."

"She won't leave the pen, Mom. How am I going to get her back home?"

"I have an idea." Mom headed off toward the house and returned a few minutes later with a cookie covered in peanut butter.

Lilyanne sniffed the air, leaped from the pen and made a beeline to Mom. As Lilyanne devoured the cookie, Mom was able to tie a rope around the dog's neck.

"Let's get her into the car," Mom said. "I'll drop her off on my way to town."

Alone with the pups, Emily spent several minutes calming them down. And then she tackled her chores. First, she emptied the wastebaskets and then stripped her bed and put the sheets in the laundry basket. Outdoor chores followed indoor chores. Emily swept the front porch and back porch and rinsed them with the hose. Three rugs hung on the clothesline, waiting for their weekly cleaning. Emily grabbed the broom and beat the dust and dirt out of them.

She finished her tasks as fast as she could and skipped to the garage. The pups followed her to the field where they went potty. Emily got a good look at them in the sunshine and didn't like what she saw.

"You're all going to have a bath," she told them. "I can't sell dirty puppies." She figured she had enough time to get them cleaned up before taking them to the grocery store.

Emily called the pups. They followed her back to the garage as Dad drove up and parked the truck. When he got out, two puppies ran over and jumped on his legs.

"That's Caramel and Bruiser," Emily said. "I'm going to give them all a bath. Want to help?"

Dad let out a big sigh and scratched his chin. "Well, I'd really like to spend some time with you. So…yes, I'll help wash the puppies after I change my clothes."

Emily beamed. "Really?"

"Yep," her dad answered. "You stay with the pups and I'll be back in a flash."

Emily hooked up the hose to rinse the puppies. She was excited to spend time with Dad. He'd been so busy lately, and she missed him when he had long trips away from home.

When Dad returned, he carried a pail of soapy water, rag towels, and a couple of Queenie's brushes. "Tricks of the trade," he said as he rolled up his sleeves and began to wash Splotches. Emily did her best to rinse the freshly scrubbed pups, but each one yelped and squirmed and tried to get away. And when they were set loose, they shook from head to toe, flinging water everywhere, and rolled in the grass.

Dad grinned. "That's better than rolling in the dirt."

By the time they'd finished washing the last puppy, they were both soaked.

"This one is Henry," Emily said as she dried him. "I

named him after Grandpa."

"Well, then, why didn't you call him Grandpa?" Dad asked.

He looked serious, and Emily giggled. "You can't name a puppy Grandpa!"

"I think you can," Dad replied.

As if on cue, Grandpa arrived. Goldie ran over and jumped against his leg.

Grandpa picked her up. "This puppy smells great!"

"She had a bath," Emily said. "They all did."

"People won't be able to resist them," Grandpa said. "Shall we head to the store and see if we can sell one, or three, or seven?"

"Or ten!" Emily said. After the words left her mouth, she wished she'd said nine.

"All right, then. Go change and I'll load the pups," Grandpa said.

Emily hurried to her room and cleaned up for the big puppy sale. A part of her felt a little sad because she'd miss the puppies once they were sold, but she was more hopeful than anything. The puppies needed good homes, and it was up to her to make sure they were safe. She pulled her hair into pigtails, skipped down the stairs and into the kitchen.

Mom added a sandwich, a one-dollar bill, four quarters and masking tape to the shoe box she would use as her money box. She then handed Emily three small FOR SALE signs.

"Thanks, Mom!"

"I wanted to have a little part in the puppy sale," Mom said. "Now remember, Dad and I are going to the city today, and Grandpa will pick you up. Good luck. I'm rooting for you."

Emily stood there, suddenly facing a wave of doubt. Could she do it? Could she sell the puppies all by herself? She couldn't disappoint Mom and Dad, or the puppies. She had to do this. Think positive, she told herself.

Emily shook off her doubts and left the house. Grandpa boosted her into the truck bed where she sat right smack in the middle of those bales of straw with those sweet-smelling puppies. Ten minutes later they pulled into the grocery store parking lot.

Grandpa called to Emily. "We'll set you up in the shade of that big Maple tree." He pointed to the right of the store.

"Shouldn't we be near the door where people can see the

puppies?" she asked.

"You won't like sitting in the sun all afternoon, and the pups won't like it either," Grandpa answered. "Let's add some arrows to the signs and hang them on the doors. That will send people your way."

Grandpa parked near the tree. While he arranged the straw pen, Emily set up a card table and chair they'd brought along. She put the shoe box on the table and taped one of her signs to the front of it. Emily stepped back and read: PUPPIES FOR SALE - $2.00

She helped put the pups inside the pen. Some of them whined and walked stiff legged as they made their way through the grass. Brownie and Pumpkin found sticks to chew on while the other pups tried to steal them.

"All set?" Grandpa asked. He set a pail of dog food and two dishes next to the straw.

Emily looked around. "Do we have water?"

Grandpa snapped his fingers. "It's in the truck." He returned a few seconds later with two glass bottles filled with water. He also handed her a book. "Your mom thought you might need something to read," he said. "I'll pick you up at five o'clock. Mr. Fripp will check on you. Let him know if you need anything else."

"Thanks, Grandpa," she said.

It was time to sell the puppies. Determination filled her heart. Today, the pups would have new homes. Emily felt positively positive.

CHAPTER 17

How Much for a Pup?

Emily waited for people to come see the puppies. And waited. And waited. Some of her neighbors waved before they went into the store. Other people entered and left without even looking her way. That's when she realized she'd forgotten to put up the other signs.

She found them under the shoe box and added arrows. Emily ran to the store doors and taped one sign on the inside, and the other one on the outside. Now both signs pointed toward the Maple tree. Heart pounding, she hurried back to her table believing people would now come see the pups.

Emily lifted Pumpkin from the pen and held her close.

"You're the cutest little thing," she cooed. "And you're my favorite."

Loud voices caused her to look up. Oh, no! The Trenton sisters, and their mother, were coming toward her. Emily cringed. Why were they here? They already had two dogs, and Emily hardly ever saw the sisters play with them. The sisters made her feel all jittery inside. She broke into a sweat and put Pumpkin down as her stomach flip-flopped.

"Well, look here girls. It's our neighbor. How are you, Emily?" Mrs. Trenton asked.

"Good," was all she could say, waiting for the sisters to start their teasing.

"My girls want to see the pups," Mrs. Trenton said. "Come on now, girls. Don't be shy."

Shy? Emily thought. They were never shy.

Sissy walked over to the pen and lifted Splotches. Carol sat on the straw and scratched Rusty under his chin.

"These puppies are adorable," Mrs. Trenton said. "Don't you think so girls?"

They didn't answer which seemed to make their mother angry.

"I asked you a question," she said with a scowl across her

face.

"Yes, mom," Sissy answered quietly.

Emily bit her lip as the sisters passed the pups back and forth. They were acting strange. It made Emily more uncomfortable than when they teased her. She wished they would leave.

"Can we get one, Mom?" Sissy asked. She pulled Rusty onto her lap.

"And who is going to take care of yet another dog?" Mrs. Trenton said. "I've got enough to do keeping you girls out of trouble."

Sissy pulled back as if slapped, and Emily had to look away. She felt sorry for them, but not sorry enough to let them buy a puppy. Their home would not be a good home. Emily reached across the table and knocked over the for-sale sign.

She rose and crossed her arms. "The puppies are ten dollars each."

"Well, good luck selling them at that price," Mrs. Trenton said. "No mutt is worth ten dollars. Come on, girls."

The sisters put the Splotches and Rusty back into the pen and followed their mother to the store. Halfway there, Carol turned and stuck out her tongue.

Emily shook her head, confused by the sisters. Were they mean because their mother was mean to them? One thing she knew for sure. She was going to pick each puppy's owner.

Not much happened for the next hour, but as the sun moved, Emily had to as well. She moved the table, chair and money box to another shady spot beneath the tree. The straw pen for the puppies was still partly in the shade so she didn't have to try and move it. After that, she ate her sandwich and took a sip of the water. Ugh! She spit it out. It tasted like watered-down milk.

Emily picked up the book Mom had sent, but before she read one page a man and woman showed up. They were followed by a younger couple with two little girls. For several minutes, Emily picked up puppies, handed them over to be examined, and then put them back into the pen. The little girls squealed and wanted all the pups. Finally, Emily's hard work paid off. The man and woman bought two puppies, and the young couple bought one.

Emily stared at the money in her hand. Six dollars! She felt good and bad at the same time. She'd sold three puppies, but her heart ached. She'd probably never see Sandy, Splotches and Brownie again.

She looked down at the seven remaining pups as they

wriggled against each other, trying to go to sleep. They were worn out from all the excitement. Emily was a little tired, too. She stretched and took a walk through the parking lot and back. She sat on a bale of straw and picked up her mystery book.

"Excuse me."

Emily looked up. A young man stood in front of her.

"How much for a puppy?" he asked.

"Two dollars," she replied.

A lady joined him, and they peered into the pen at the same time.

"Oh, John," she said. "Could they be any cuter?"

"We're only looking, Debbie. Not buying," John answered.

Emily put the book down. "Would you like to hold one?"

"Please. I love dogs," Debbie said.

Emily handed her Rusty first, then Sarah, followed by the other pups, one at a time. It took ten minutes for her to decide to buy Sarah.

"She needs me," Debbie insisted.

Emily agreed. "I can tell she likes you."

John shook his head, laughed, and gave Emily the money.

As Sarah was carried off, Emily felt another twinge of sadness. She had to remind herself Sarah had a new home. *Think positive! And be happy.*

Emily picked up her book again.

***

"Young lady? Are you all right?"

Emily heard words, but they were mumbled and sounded far away. She opened her eyes, sat up and looked around. Oops. She'd fallen asleep and now two elderly people stared at her.

"I'm sorry. Did you come to buy a puppy?"

"Perhaps," the man said. "I'm Sam O'Neill. This is my wife, Ginny."

"I want a dog that will bark at strangers," Ginny said.

"Well, the pups bark, but I don't know if they'll bark at strangers," Emily said. "They are two dollars each."

Sam frowned. "I have one dollar to spend."

Emily hesitated, but she liked the man and his wife. They seemed kind, and Emily felt a puppy would have a good home with them. Ginny finally decided on Bruiser, and Emily agreed to sell him for half price.

"Thank you," Sam said. "You are kind to lower the price."

"You're welcome," she replied with a big smile. It felt right to sell Bruiser for a dollar.

After Sam and Ginny left, Emily counted her money. Nine dollars. She wondered how she would make up the extra dollar to give Mr. Brock. She should have thought about that sooner.

During the next hour Emily grew restless. She tried to read her book but couldn't concentrate. The five remaining pups whined a lot and tried to climb out of the pen. Emily took each one on a short walk, gave them food and water and they calmed down.

After that, Mr. Fripp paid her a visit. "It's three-fifteen, Emily. I thought you could use a snack." He handed her a small bag of crackers and a grape soda.

"Thanks. I can pay you." She had the quarters in the money box.

"No, no," Mr. Fripp said. "This is my treat. How's it going? I saw you had some customers."

"I sold five puppies."

"Wonderful. I hope you sell the rest of them. I've got to

get back to work, but please let me know if you need anything else."

"I will. Thanks, Mr. Fripp," she said.

Emily finished the crackers and soda. She glanced at the pups. They were back asleep, piled on top of each other. She picked up her book again.

A horn tooted and startled Emily. Her book went sailing. She looked up and there was Grandpa, waving at her. He parked his truck and ambled over.

"You don't have to throw things at me." He picked up the book and handed it Emily.

"You scared me!"

He laughed. "So, tell me how the puppy sale is going."

"I sold five puppies," Emily said. "That's pretty good, right?"

"That's very good!" He patted her on the shoulder. "Five pups have new homes."

"Is it time to leave?" Emily hoped not. She would still like to sell another puppy.

"Not yet. I'll sit with you for the last half hour. Let's see what we can do together."

Grandpa was like a circus ringmaster. "Come one, come all; the puppies do call. They call to you, 'How do you do?'"

Emily doubled over with laughter, her sides aching.

Shoppers entering and leaving the store heard his singsong. People laughed, some waved, and some came over for a peek at the pups.

After a while, Grandpa looked at his watch. "Well, we gave it a good try. Your mom and dad should be back from the city. How about we pack up?"

"Hey, Henry."

Grandpa turned. "Well, howdy, Dave." They shook hands. "This is my granddaughter, Emily."

Dave shook her hand, too. "What do you have here?" He bent down and lifted a pup.

"That's Rusty," she said.

Dave held Rusty at eye level and studied him from side to side, and top to bottom. "A fine-looking pup if I ever saw one," he said. "Mr. Fripp is my uncle. He told me to get over here fast and see these pups. How much are they?"

"Two dollars," Emily answered.

Dave took his time examining each puppy, but in the end

he decided on Rusty and paid Emily.

"Time to pack up," Grandpa said. Dave helped them put everything in the truck bed while Emily got to hold Rusty one last time. On the way home, Emily checked her shoe box again, and counted the puppy money. She had $11.00. Maybe she could use the dollar Mom had given her for change. If she did, that would equal $12.00. Exactly what she needed.

"A penny for your thoughts," Grandpa said.

Emily sighed. "I'm thinking about Sandy, Splotches, Brownie, Sarah, Bruiser, and Rusty. I hope they'll be happy in their new homes."

Grandpa reached over and ruffled her hair. "They are going to be very happy. And, at this rate, I think you'll probably sell the rest of them by next weekend."

Emily gulped. All of them? She loved the puppies so much. What would she do when they were all sold?

As if reading her thoughts, Grandpa said, "I know you're going to miss them, but this is the best thing for them. Finding good homes ensures that they are all taken care of. You'll feel really proud when that happens."

She sure hoped Grandpa was right.

CHAPTER 18

A Second Chance

Sunday morning, after church, Emily changed into a short-sleeved shirt and shorts and bounded down the stairs. She had to get back to the grocery store. Mr. Fripp had called last night and said people wanted to see the pups. Dad was going to take her to the store, and she didn't want to be late.

"Slow down, Emily," Mom said. "You need to eat lunch before you go."

"I'm not hungry," she said as the screened door slammed behind her. She plopped on the steps and slipped into her shoes.

Emily helped Dad load everything in the back of his work

truck. Before they could leave the driveway, Mom ran down the steps and handed Emily a sandwich and thermos of water.

"Can't let you go without food. You know that."

"Thanks, Mom."

They arrived at the store at noon and set up again under the shade of the same Maple tree. Emily put the signs back on the store doors.

"Mom will pick you up around three-thirty," Dad said. "If you get done sooner, ask Mr. Fripp to call her."

"I will," Emily answered.

Knowing people were interested, and would be coming, made her feel a little bolder. She called to a few people, asking if they wanted to see the puppies. She took turns holding Caramel, Goldie, Pumpkin and Henry so people would get a good look at them.

Mr. Fripp stopped by. "Have the Boltens arrived yet?"

Emily shook her head.

"Don't worry. They'll be here soon."

Emily waited and waited. Finally, a family of four stopped and looked at the pups.

"Hi," the woman said. "We're the Boltens. Mr. Fripp said

you had adorable pups for sale. We've been thinking a long time about getting a dog."

The girl picked up Caramel and buried her face in the pup's neck. "She's soft."

When the boy wrestled Pumpkin from the straw pen, Emily held her breath. *Please don't pick Pumpkin.*

"Let's take them both," the boy said.

The father shook his head. "Only one and that's final."

"I'd hoped for a female," the mother said. "Female dogs are more devoted, and they're easier to train."

Emily wondered if the lady was right.

While the two kids fought over which one to buy, their father decided by the flip of a coin. Caramel ended up the winner. The boy was mad and stalked off. But Emily breathed a sigh of relief. For now, Pumpkin was safe.

The man opened his wallet. "I believe the price is two dollars?"

Emily hesitated. She had thought to raise the price, but with everyone looking at her, she gulped and said, "You're right. Two dollars it is."

The girl, full of smiles, carried Caramel as they walked to

their car. Emily collapsed into the chair. Henry, Goldie, and Pumpkin settled down for a nap.

Emily spent some time reading, but soon became stiff from sitting. A walk around the tree several times made her feel better. Then she exercised the pups. Then boredom set in. She needed something else to do to pass the time. She didn't want to be caught napping again.

Luckily, a station wagon pulled up and a woman leaned out the window.

"Do you have any puppies left?"

"Yes. I have three," Emily said.

The woman parked the car and hurried over. "My mother and father bought one yesterday and my husband fell in love with it. His birthday is this weekend. Guess what he's getting?"

"A puppy?"

"Yes." The woman clapped her hands. "One dollar, right?"

Emily gulped. Yesterday's good deed had come back to haunt her.

"Ah, yes. One dollar."

The woman clapped again. "Wonderful. You do have a male pup, don't you?"

Emily nodded and picked up the last male pup. "I named him Henry, after my Grandpa, but you can rename him if you want to."

The woman paid her, and Emily handed over Henry.

"Goodness. He's even cuter than Sebastian."

"Who's Sebastian?" Emily asked.

"The pup you sold my father."

Emily almost laughed out loud. Bruiser was now Sebastian.

The next family who came by spent time petting the puppies, but in the end decided not to buy one. Emily asked the man for the time, and learned it was already three o'clock. Mom would be there in a half hour, and she still had two pups to sell. She reached down, scooped up Goldie and Pumpkin and held them close.

Goldie chewed Emily's hair as Pumpkin licked her face. It was quiet with eight pups gone. She missed them, but had to think of them in loving homes with someone to play with. She buried her face between the pups until they squirmed to be put down.

When she looked up again, a little boy, maybe six years old, stood there staring at the puppies.

"Do you want to hold one?" Emily asked.

The boy nodded, but when she handed him Goldie he began to cry.

"Hey, what's the matter?" she asked.

The little boy tried to speak through his sobs. "M-m-m-my dog. Sh-she died."

"Oh, I'm sorry," Emily said. Her heart ached for him.

A man joined the boy, bent down and said, "It's okay, son. You can cry over Lady. She was your best friend."

Goldie licked the boy's face and his eyes widened. "I want this puppy, Daddy. I love him."

"Um, she's a girl puppy," Emily said.

The boy sniffed and whipped his nose on his shirt sleeve. "I love her."

"How much for the pup?" the man asked.

"Two dollars."

"Hmm." The man opened his wallet. "I don't have cash with me. Will you take a check?"

Emily wasn't sure what to do. She didn't know much about checks, but she could see the boy needed Goldie.

"The puppy is free," Emily said.

The man looked surprised. "Are you sure?"

Emily nodded. "I know she'll have a good home with you."

"You are very kind," he said. "And you've made Brian happy."

Brian's smile was huge. Almost bigger than his face. "I'm going to call her Lady."

"Lady is a wonderful name," Emily said.

A happy boy left with his puppy. Emily picked up Pumpkin and received a slobbering of puppy kisses. She wiped her face with her arm as Pumpkin snuggled in her lap, chewed on her fingers, and completely stole Emily's heart.

Nine puppies had new homes, and now, more than anything, all Emily wanted in return was Pumpkin.

She wished she knew how to make it happen.

CHAPTER 19

Decision Time

As she waited for Mom to pick her up, Emily packed up all the puppy sale items and put them inside the straw pen. She ran to the store doors and removed the for-sale signs. All the while she had been thinking up ideas on how she could keep Pumpkin. But none of her ideas seemed like they would work. She was so caught up in her thoughts, she didn't even hear Mom drive up.

"Sorry I'm late," Mom said, as she got out of the car. "How'd you do today?"

"I sold three puppies. Pumpkin is the only one left," Emily replied. She held up Pumpkin for Mom to see.

"I'm so proud of you, Emily. Nine puppies! Wow. You

did great. I think we should have a celebration when we get home."

Emily like that idea. She put Pumpkin in the back seat, jabbering on about Henry, Goldie, and Caramel and the people who bought them. Then she helped Mom load the car. Everything went inside, except the bales of straw which couldn't fit.

"Looks like Grandpa will have to pick them up," Mom said.

They headed home, Pumpkin on Emily's lap. She couldn't hold her wish inside any longer. "Mom, I want to keep Pumpkin. We're meant to be together."

Mom smiled, "I'm not surprised, so I'll tell you this much. I'll talk to your father. No promises, but we will discuss it."

Emily smiled. "Thanks, Mom." She snuggled Pumpkin against her neck and prayed her parents would say yes.

At home, Emily put an old blanket in the front hallway along with a bowl of water and a bowl of mushed up dog food. Right away Pumpkin spilled her water dish. Emily ran for a towel. As she wiped up the spill Pumpkin bit the towel and wouldn't let go.

Emily laughed. "You're a silly puppy. Water is for

drinking and towels are for wiping."

Pumpkin stared up at her, wriggling from side to side. She barked.

"Wash up for dinner," Mom called.

Emily did so and joined her parents. Pumpkin sprawled on her feet. After Mom said grace, Emily passed the rolls to Dad. He took the basket, set it on the table next to him and looked at Emily.

"Your mother told me you sold all the pups, except for one," he said.

Emily nodded.

"Well, I want you to know I think you're amazing. You put your mind to this task and followed it through. All except for Pumpkin."

Emily nodded again.

"And you're supposed to take her back to Mr. Brock?"

"Yes," she said softly.

Dad picked up a roll. "Why not sell Pumpkin to yourself?"

Emily stared at him.

"You've shown us you're ready for a dog and all the

responsibility that goes with it," Mom added. "We've agreed you can buy Pumpkin."

Emily jumped up and danced around the table. She hugged Mom. She hugged Dad. And she bear-hugged Grandpa as he entered the room.

"Hey, what's all the fuss about?" Grandpa asked.

"I get to keep Pumpkin!" Emily squealed.

"Great," Grandpa said. "You get to keep a pumpkin. Isn't it a bit early for Halloween?"

"Oh, Grandpa." Emily chased Pumpkin around the room until she caught her. "You're mine, mine, MINE!" she said to the pup and she skipped back to the kitchen. "Can we go see Mr. Brock right now?"

"Slow down, sweetie," Mom said. "Let's have our dinner first. I'm not even sure Winston is home yet. Have you seen him, Henry?"

"Sure have," Grandpa said. "He got back this afternoon. He looks rested. He told me he's mighty thankful for all the help with the dogs."

Emily kissed Pumpkin and put her down. She slid into her chair next to Grandpa.

Mom pointed to the bathroom. "Wash again."

***

After dinner, Emily took Pumpkin upstairs to her room. She didn't want the pup out of her sight. She took the dollar bills from the money box and counted them. She had $16.00 total. Subtracting the dollar and four quarters Mom had given her for change, she had only $14.00. She'd sold nine puppies for $14.00. Her heart took a dive and tangled with her stomach as the truth hit her. What would Mr. Brock say?

She grabbed her piggy bank from the dresser and emptied it on the bed. The dimes, quarters, nickels and pennies totaled $2.75. When she added it to the puppy money, she now had $16.75; still not enough to pay Mr. Brock. She needed $18.00 for the pups she sold, and $2.00 for Pumpkin. How would she make up the difference?

Emily lay next to the puppy. "I'm in big trouble. I hope Mr. Brock will let me buy you."

She got up, stuffed the money into her pocket and took Pumpkin downstairs. It was time to ask for help.

Emily went to the kitchen. No one was there. She pushed open the screen door and stepped onto the porch.

"Mom? Dad?" No answer. "Grandpa? Where are you?"

He came out of the garage. "Your parents went for a walk.

Are you ready to go?"

"Um, sure," Emily said. "I needed to talk with them first."

"You don't seem happy, and a moment ago you were over the moon."

Emily looked down, stirring the dirt with her shoe. "I have a problem."

"Out with it then. Let's find the solution."

They sat on the steps, and Emily took a deep breath. "I sold two puppies for a dollar each, and I gave Goldie away for free to a little boy whose dog died. And now I don't have enough money to pay Mr. Brock, or to buy Pumpkin."

Grandpa rubbed his chin. "Definitely a problem. How much do you have?"

"Fourteen dollars from the sale, and $2.75 in my piggy bank. Oh, and $2.00 from Mom, but I haven't asked if I can have it."

"Hmm," Grandpa said. "What are your options?"

Emily turned toward him. "I need to borrow the rest of the money. I'll work hard to pay it back. You know I will. Help me, Grandpa."

"There is another option," he said.

"There is?"

"Tell Mr. Brock the truth and see what he says. He may accept the amount you collected. Didn't think of that, did you?"

Emily shook her head. Not telling the truth had gotten her into a lot of trouble lately. She guessed it couldn't hurt to try.

"Thanks Grandpa. You're the best."

He chuckled. "Let's go and see what happens."

A few minutes later they turned into Mr. Brock's driveway. Emily held Pumpkin too tight and the pup yipped.

"Better give her some breathing room," Grandpa said with a laugh. "You want her alive, don't you?"

The truck lurched to a stop. Emily opened the door and slid to the ground. Pumpkin squirmed in her arms and wanted to get down. "No, Pumpkin. Be a good puppy right now." She followed Grandpa, and they walked up the steps.

A picnic basket sat next to the front door covered with a checkered dish towel. Grandpa shook his head. "This is the second basket today."

"What's in the baskets?" Emily asked.

"Food, mostly. Comfort food some would call it."

Good food to make you feel good, Emily thought. She liked that.

Grandpa knocked, and Emily called out, "Mr. Brock! It's Emily and Grandpa."

Through the screen door, Emily saw her neighbor shuffle toward them. He leaned heavily on his cane. He pushed open the door and stepped outside. "Hello. What brings you by today?"

"Got some news for you," Grandpa said.

"Well, let's sit here in the shade. Weather's nice enough." Slowly, Mr. Brock lowered himself into a chair. "I've been wondering about those puppies. How are they doing?"

"Emily's worked really hard to sell them," Grandpa said. "I'll let her do the talking."

She leaned against the house, feeling nervous and excited at the same time. Pumpkin squirmed, and she put her down. "I sold all the puppies, except for this one. They went to good homes. I'm sure of it."

"Thank you for your hard work," Mr. Brock said. "I appreciate it."

She pulled the dollar bills from her left pocket and handed them to Mr. Brock. "I got $14.00 for nine puppies." She waited for him to count the money, but he didn't. "I know it's not enough, but there's a good reason why. I also have $2.75 from my piggy bank." She dug into her right pocket and came up with her change.

"You never mind about the money," he said. "It doesn't matter now. You sold most of the puppies, and I'm glad there's one left. I think I'll keep this one and train it."

Keep a puppy? Emily's stomach lurched. *But that would be Pumpkin.* She was about to say something when Grandpa put a hand on her arm.

"Why do you want this puppy, Winston?" he asked. "You said the pups were mutts. That's why you let Emily sell them."

"Knight's getting pretty old. I'll train this one to take his place, and when Paul comes home the pup will keep him busy. He can finish her training."

Emily's stomach clenched. *When Paul comes home? Paul is missing. What if he doesn't come home?*

"N-N-o," she stammered. "My parents said I could buy her. Tell him, Grandpa."

"She's ready for her own dog," Grandpa said. "And she's set her mind on Pumpkin."

Mr. Brock didn't answer.

"Emily's worked hard," Grandpa continued. "She sold the puppies. She helped take care of your hunting dogs. I think it's fair to let her have Pumpkin."

Mr. Brock shifted in his chair, winced and rubbed his leg. "You're right, Henry, it would be fair. But I can't let the pup go. Paul's going to come home. I have to keep her, for him."

Emily grabbed Pumpkin and began to back away, but Grandpa steered her to one side of the porch. "Emmy. Right now, Mr. Brock believes he needs Pumpkin. He might change his mind, but we can't force him to, and we can't take the pup."

Emily pushed Pumpkin into Grandpa's arms and then ran to the truck. She couldn't breathe. Couldn't breathe at all. She sucked in air and tried to calm down. *Oh, Pumpkin!*

Grandpa talked to her on the way home, but Emily didn't respond. She was numb.

When they arrived home, Emily fled to her room and fell upon the bed. She felt empty with nothing to fill the void inside her. If only Grandpa had never mentioned those puppies. If only she'd never seen them. But she had, and she'd fallen in love with them. And now they were all gone, even Pumpkin. She'd never felt more miserable in her life.

***

"Emily. Wake up, honey."

Mom's voice. Mom's calling.

Emily opened her eyes. The light from the hallway spilled into her room.

"Is it time to get up?" she asked.

"No, dear. It's still night."

Emily turned toward the wall.

"I'm sorry, sweetie," Mom said. "I know this must seem quite unfair. Do you want to talk about it?"

Emily shook her head. She couldn't think. She wanted to go back to sleep.

"We'll talk in the morning," Mom whispered.

Emily barely heard her.

CHAPTER 20

The Truth Hurts

When Emily woke the next morning, she felt sick and sore all over. She could barely drag herself out of bed. Red, swollen eyes greeted her in the bathroom mirror. If only she could go back to bed and pull the covers over her head. She dressed slowly, and halfway made her bed. As she gathered her clothes for the laundry, she caught a whiff of puppy. Her shirt smelled like Pumpkin, sweet and cuddly.

Emily threw it to the floor. Because of Mr. Brock, she would never have Pumpkin. Why did he need another hunting dog when he already had four? Why couldn't he see she needed Pumpkin?

"Up and at it," Mom called out. "We need to talk before you leave for the bus."

Emily shuffled downstairs and slumped at the table. She picked at her toast and cereal while Mom washed dishes and chattered on about what a beautiful day it would be.

"Emily?"

Startled, she looked up. "What?"

"I'm really sorry this happened," Mom said. "I was surprised to hear Mr. Brock decided to keep Pumpkin. But I do believe that some problems need extra time to work themselves out."

A lump formed in Emily's throat and she had a hard time swallowing past it. She knew Mom was trying hard to help her feel better, but it wasn't working. Nothing would work except keeping Pumpkin.

Emily pushed back from the table and gathered her books and sack lunch. Before she could duck out of the kitchen, Mom wrapped her in a big hug.

"Try to have a good day, honey."

Emily trudged to the road and got there as the bus pulled up. She climbed aboard. Her spirits lifted a little when she saw an empty seat next to Jimmy Coates who, as usual, was sleeping. She asked Mr. Allen if she could sit there instead of in her assigned seat.

Mr. Allen nodded. "Okay for today. The Hobart kids are out sick."

Emily slid into the seat beside Jimmy. She closed her eyes and laid her head back. The bus rattled on down the road picking up kids. She knew when the Trenton sisters got on the bus because Carol was so loud. As they walked by, Carol bumped into Emily and it wasn't by accident. A little while later something wet smacked Emily's cheek. She jerked upright and looked around. She spied a small wad of paper on the seat. A spit wad. Yucky.

She turned and caught sight of Sissy and Carol. Carol glared at her, but Sissy was looking out the window. Emily sighed. Mom and Greg both said to be extra nice to them, but she didn't have the energy to do so. She faced the front of the bus and closed her eyes.

"Wake up, teeny weenie," Carol taunted. "How come you're not blabbing over those stupid puppies? Dog got your tongue?" She laughed loudly.

Anger threatened to burst forth, but Emily fought it back.

"Quiet down back there!" Mr. Allen yelled.

In the seat ahead of her, Jeff Brown turned and whispered, "Did you sell the pups?"

Emily nodded. "No more puppies to worry about." She looked out the window and wished that everyone would leave her alone.

***

Emily heard the same questions many times that day.

"What happened to the puppies?"

"Did you sell the puppies?"

"How many puppies did you sell?"

She stuck to her story that she sold them all. Each time she told the lie, it got a little easier. So how come she felt worse?

Between classes she told Sarah bits and pieces of what happened with Mr. Brock, but there wasn't time for the whole story until lunch. They took their lunch sacks outside, raced to one side of the playground and sat in the grass. Emily told her everything.

Sarah's eyes widened. "I can't believe he kept Pumpkin after all you did. He's awful."

Emily was glad her cousin said that. It felt okay to be mad

at Mr. Brock when someone else felt the same way.

"He can't take care of Pumpkin. He's still using a cane to get around," Emily said.

"Do you think he will train her?"

Emily shrugged. "He might, but what if he can't? What if Pumpkin doesn't like to hunt?" She stopped talking, afraid to speak her other thoughts.

"What's wrong?" Sarah asked.

"What if Paul doesn't come home and Mr. Brock gets tired of Pumpkin?"

They were silent for a few seconds.

"Are you going to fight for her?" Sarah asked, her fists punching the air as a pretend fighter.

Emily stared at her. *Fight for Pumpkin? If she did, maybe Mr. Brock would realize how much she wanted her, needed her.*

"What would I say?" Emily asked.

Sarah thrust her shoulders from side to side. "Mr. Brock? You're a grouch and I want Pumpkin."

Emily couldn't help but giggle. "Or I could say, 'I took care of your dogs. Now give me Pumpkin!'"

"How about this?" Sarah said. "Give up the mutt or I'll steal her again."

They doubled over in laughter, but Emily knew she couldn't say any of those things. She did feel braver, though, braver than before.

"You could spy on Pumpkin every day. Then you would know, for sure, if he's taking care of her," Sarah said.

Emily nodded. "But I'd want to grab her and take her home."

"Could you get a different puppy? I'll check the newspaper ads for you."

Emily wrapped her arms around her knees and rocked back and forth. "Right now, I only want Pumpkin."

The bell rang and the girls jumped up. Sarah locked arms with Emily. "We'll think of something."

Emily frowned. She'd heard that before.

When she got on the bus after school, Mr. Allen told her the Trenton sisters had been kicked off for two days. Emily tried not to smile as she moved down the aisle. But she whooped silently as she slid into the seat. Her own space for two days!

She scooted to the window and spread her books and

homework next to her. It felt great to have the extra room. She hummed to herself. She could sing or read or stare out the window or talk to the girl across the aisle if she wanted to. Nobody would pick on her.

Carol deserved it, she thought. She should have been kicked off for a month! But Sissy? Emily felt a little sorry for her. Sissy had been nicer lately.

***

After dinner, Emily carried the dishes to the sink. Pumpkin was the only thing on her mind. She'd made an important decision and was ready to share it. She turned to speak, but noticed Dad peering at her over the evening paper.

"What?" Emily said.

"I think it's best you stay away from that pup," he said.

Emily's mouth went dry. She'd been about to tell them she'd fight to win Pumpkin back. And he wanted her to stay away?

"I can't do that," Emily said.

"If you want to look for another dog, we will," he added.

"I don't want another dog, Dad! I want Pumpkin."

"It's time to let your heart heal," Mom added. "And Mr.

Brock needs space to get to know Pumpkin."

"He can't take care of her, and when he realizes that, he'll give Pumpkin to me," Emily said. She looked to Grandpa for help. "Tell them, Grandpa!"

"Emily's right. The pup will be a lot of work for Winston. His other dogs still need care, and I'm going to continue helping him until his leg heals. But I can't do that alone. I need Emily. That means she'll see Pumpkin now and then."

Emily stared at her parents. "I'm not giving up on Pumpkin."

Tension filled the kitchen. Things said and left unsaid hung heavy in the room. Dad shook his head, stood and went outside. Grandpa followed. Emily dried the dishes while Mom put them away. After that, she went upstairs to her room to rest, but her mind whirled and twirled. Why couldn't her parents see how much she needed Pumpkin? No matter what, she wouldn't stay away.

A knock on the door startled her, and then Dad leaned in.

"This is quite a puppy predicament," he said. "Your mom and I didn't mean to upset you with our comments. But we need to consider Mr. Brock's feelings. Can I ask you a question?"

She didn't answer.

"Emily?"

"Yes?"

"Think about this. What would you do if you were Mr. Brock? Would you keep the puppy for someone you love, or would you give it away?"

Emily swallowed a lump rising in her throat. *Maybe the pup means hope to Mr. Brock; hope that Paul will come back home. Maybe holding on to Pumpkin is holding on to Paul?*

"I'd keep Pumpkin," she answered honestly.

CHAPTER 21

Letting Go

In the garden, after school on Friday, Emily shucked sweet corn and faced the fact that she was miserable without Pumpkin. The pup had been on her mind all week – before school, during school, after school, and when she tried to go to asleep. She looked toward Mr. Brock's farm, wondering what Pumpkin was doing that very second. She'd seen Pumpkin two times during the week, but never had a chance to play with her. Seeing wasn't enough. Emily had to hold Pumpkin, and it had to happen now.

She finished her task, took the ears of corn inside and washed the silk off them. It was time to make her getaway.

"Ok if I ride my bike?" Emily asked.

Mom glanced up from the roast she was preparing for dinner. "Sure. Thanks for shucking the corn."

Emily flew out the door and jumped on her bike. She soared down the road with the wind in her face. She slowed as she turned into her neighbor's driveway and coasted past the house. Mr. Brock wasn't home. Emily peddled to the dog kennel.

Sir Taylor, Dandy Lady and Lilyanne greeted her with lots of barking. Knight wasn't there. Pumpkin wasn't there, either. Emily stepped inside the pen and petted Lilyanne.

"Hi girl. Do you know where Pumpkin is?"

Lilyanne whined and pushed her nose under Emily's hand.

"All your pups have good homes now. Even Pumpkin. I hope you get to see her a lot."

She left them and went to the chicken coop. No Pumpkin. Emily entered the big barn. Pumpkin wasn't inside. Emily peered into the small sheds around the farmyard, peeked under the shrubs, and looked all around the farmhouse. No puppy.

Emily had nowhere else to look except inside the house, and she couldn't without being invited in. Hopefully, if Mr. Brock returned, he'd tell her where Pumpkin was. Maybe she'd have time to play with her.

She returned to the hunting dogs to see if they needed food or water. Their dishes were empty. As she pumped water from the well, Emily saw a mound of dirt at the end of the garden. She didn't remember it being there before. She walked over and felt the mound. It was damp. A shovel lay nearby, and everything reminded her of when they'd buried Queenie.

She fell to her knees and her stomach knotted in pain. Old rumors made their way back into her mind. Could it be Pumpkin's grave? No! It couldn't be. Mr. Brock said he would train her to be a hunter.

A door slammed. Emily turned toward the sound. *Mr. Brock?* She sprinted to the driveway, stopping abruptly as her neighbor lifted Pumpkin from the passenger seat. A huge lump welled in her throat and her voice was stuck between sorrow and relief.

"Emily! Are you all right?" Mr. Brock said.

She shook her head. "There's a grave near the garden."

"Yes," he said. "It's Knight's grave."

"Knight died? How?"

Mr. Brock wiped his eyes with his handkerchief. "He stopped eating. I was going to take him to the vet today, but

182

he passed away last night. Your grandpa helped me bury him."

Pumpkin struggled in Mr. Brock's arms. He put her on the ground, and she scampered to Emily, who immediately scooped her up.

She breathed into Pumpkin's neck. "You're alive."

"You don't look well," Mr. Brock said.

"I thought the grave was Pumpkin's." She sniffed.

"Pumpkin's? Now why would you think that? I told you I was going to train her to hunt."

For the first time Emily really believed him. She stumbled to her feet. "I have to go now." She ran to her bike, wanting to be anywhere but there. Pumpkin followed her.

"Put her in the house for me," Mr. Brock called out.

Emily rushed Pumpkin to the house, then jumped on her bike and peddled home. Knight's death made her sad. He was a good old dog. She thought about Mr. Brock and Pumpkin, Knight and Paul. About Greg. About good and bad, truth and lies. She'd never thought about so many things at one time.

The minute Emily stepped inside the house, her mom rushed over. "Something happened. I can tell by your face."

"Knight died."

"Oh dear," Mom said. "Winston doesn't need another sorrow right now."

"I saw a grave and thought Pumpkin was buried there. But then Mr. Brock came home, and he had Pumpkin with him. He told me Knight died. Mom, he was telling the truth when he said he's going to train Pumpkin to be a hunter. I didn't believe him, but now I do." She wiped her nose with her shirt.

Mom pulled a tissue from her pocket and handed it over. "He's not a mean person, honey. He's all alone and worried for Paul."

"I know," Emily said. "I felt the same way about the puppies. I didn't know if they would be safe. But they went to good homes, and Pumpkin will have a good home with Mr. Brock and Paul."

"I'm glad you understand," Mom said.

They shared a long hug; one Emily didn't want to end.

***

After dinner dishes were put away, Emily retrieved the wagon she'd stashed in the weeds beside the old machinery barn. She loaded it with rocks and stones and pulled it to Queenie's grave. She used the larger rocks to make an outline of a heart on top of the dirt and filled the center with smaller rocks.

When she finished, she sat and wrapped her arms around her legs.

"Greg's coming home soon, Queenie. When he finds out you died, he'll be sad. But I'll tell him what a good dog you were. The best dog."

Waiting for her brother to come home was hard. Waiting to tell him the truth about Queenie was even harder.

CHAPTER 22

Healing a Heart

Saturday morning arrived, full of sunshine. Emily finished her chores by lunchtime. She ate with Mom and Dad, and then wandered around the yard with no plans for the day. She lay in the grass by the tire swing, staring at the sky. How would she fill her time when it had been all about Pumpkin, and the hunting dogs, for the past few weeks?

Sighing, she rolled on her stomach. She was glad that she'd let go of her anger toward Mr. Brock. She was only able to do that because she truly believed he would be good to Pumpkin.

So, what to do? She could gather apples and help Mom make a pie. She could visit Queenie's grave. Or maybe she'd just lie around and wait for the mailman to see if he had letters from Greg. They still didn't know when he would be coming home.

A door slammed. Emily sat up and saw Dad leave the house. She walked over to him.

"Where are you going?"

"I've got a few errands to do in town," he said.

"Can I go?"

"My first stop is a haircut. Are you sure you want to tag along?"

Emily nodded.

"Okay," Dad said. "Let your mother know."

Emily ran to the house and told Mom, then climbed into the truck. It was a beautiful autumn day and Dad drove slowly. As they passed Mr. Brock's farm, she stuck her head out the window. The wind whipped her hair as she hoped to catch sight of one of his dogs.

"What are you looking for?" Dad asked.

"Oh, nothing," Emily said.

"A Pumpkin puppy, I'll bet," he teased.

Suddenly, Dad hit the brakes and a dog darted from the

front of truck.

"I think that's Sissy's dog, Molly," Emily said.

"Where'd she go?"

Emily pointed to Mr. Brock's house. "She's over there. Molly shouldn't be this far from home."

Dad backed up and turned into the driveway.

"There she is!" Emily pointed again, this time toward Mr. Brock's garden. "It's Molly. I'm sure of it."

But Molly wasn't alone. Mr. Brock's hunting dogs were out and had Molly surrounded. Molly looked frightened. Dad whistled and got the attention of Lilyanne, Dandy Lady and Sir Taylor. As the dogs ran to him, Emily crossed the yard and grabbed the piece of rope tied around Molly's neck.

Dad and Emily led the dogs back to the kennel.

"Good thing you saw Molly," Dad said. "It's not like Winston to let his dogs out of the kennel and then leave them alone. Let's see what's going on."

They headed to the house. Emily held tight to Molly's rope. As they came to the front yard, they saw Mr. Brock. He lay on the ground near the porch. Dad ran to him, and she followed.

They knelt beside their neighbor. Dad touched his shoulder. "Winston, what happened?"

No answer.

Dad jiggled Mr. Brock's arm. "Talk to me. Are you hurt?"

"I don't think so," Mr. Brock finally answered, but he seemed to have trouble breathing. "I – I landed on my hip when I fell."

"How long have you been here?

Mr. Brock rubbed his hip. "I don't know."

"Let's see if you can sit up. Emily, take hold of his hand and slowly pull him toward you." Emily helped ease Mr. Brock into a sitting position.

"Tell me what happened," Dad said. "How did you fall?"

"I lost my balance after I let the dogs out. That's all I remember."

"Do you think you can stand?" Dad asked.

"Maybe. I'll need my cane. It's on the porch."

"I'll get it," Emily said. She handed Molly's rope to Dad. When she returned, they helped Mr. Brock to his feet, and he took hold of his cane.

"I'm going to get him to the house, Emily. I'd like you to

water the hunting dogs and then come back."

"I will," she said. And then it dawned on her. All the dogs were accounted for except one. "Mr. Brock, where's Pumpkin?"

He pointed to the house. "She's inside." He leaned on her dad as they walked to the porch.

Emily watered the dogs as fast as she could then led Molly to the house. As she walked through Mr. Brock's front door, she couldn't believe her eyes. The room looked like a wild wind had swooshed through it. Couch cushions had been pulled off, rugs twisted, and newspapers chewed. And then she smelled something all too familiar. Puppy pee.

Mr. Brock rested on the couch, one arm over his face.

"What happened to your room?" she asked.

"Pup's got too much energy. I had to confine her to the back bedroom."

Pumpkin confined? Emily couldn't stand the thought. "I'll take her out to play."

"I'd appreciate it," he said. "I was going to let her play with the other dogs. That was before I fell. She's calmer after she goes outside."

"She had nine brothers and sisters, and now she's alone."

After the words left her mouth, Emily held her breath. She shouldn't have said anything, even if it was the truth.

There was an awkward silence between them before he answered. "Dog's not alone. She has me."

Emily breathed again. "I'll take her out now."

Dad came back to the room. "I spoke to Bill Trenton. He's on his way to pick up Molly."

Wow, Emily said to herself. Mr. Trenton's home! That's great news. Sissy and Carol would be thrilled to have their dad back.

Suddenly, loud barking came from the back of the house. Emily led Molly through the house to the bedrooms. She opened the door where the barking came from and her mouth fell open. The room was a mess, the same as the living room. Maybe worse.

Pumpkin leaped from the bed, straight into her arms.

"I'm glad to see you, too." Emily cuddled Pumpkin, but then gently scolded her. "What a mess you've made. I can't believe you did this." She bent over and let Pumpkin see Molly. The dogs wagged tails and licked each other.

"Let's go play," she said.

Pumpkin was a bolt of energy once her feet touched the

grass. The pup darted around Emily, and bit at her shoelaces. Molly didn't seem to know how to act around crazy Pumpkin, so Emily kept Molly close. She didn't want her to run away again.

A car pulled up. As soon as it stopped Sissy jumped out and ran to Molly. She fell to her knees and threw her arms around her dog.

"Molly, oh Molly. I thought I'd lost you," she cried.

"Thanks for finding her," Mr. Trenton said as he joined them. "The girls looked everywhere."

"You're welcome," Emily said.

"I'm going to check on Mr. Brock," he said. "I won't be long."

"Okay, Dad." Sissy hugged Molly fiercely. As the silence grew, Emily knew she had to say something.

"I'll bet you're glad your dad's home."

Sissy nodded.

"And I'm sorry you got kicked off the bus."

She shrugged. "It's Carol's fault."

"She's kind of scary when she gets mean," Emily said.

Sissy looked up. "Carol's mean to everyone, even me."

Emily remembered the bus incident when the sisters had fought.

"I'm sorry I picked on you," Sissy said.

"But you've been nicer lately. I've noticed."

Sissy didn't answer.

"Maybe we could be friends?" Emily asked.

Sissy nodded again.

"Um, that's great," Emily replied. It was a start.

After Mr. Trenton and Sissy headed home, Dad called Emily to the porch. "You might as well head home. I'm going to stay with Mr. Brock for a while."

"What should I do with Pumpkin? She can't go back into the bedroom, Dad. It's a mess. Worse than the living room."

Dad scratched his chin, thinking. "Put her in the chicken coop. When Grandpa gets here, we'll figure out what to do."

Reluctantly, Emily took the pup to the coop. She snuggled her one more time before putting her inside.

"Be a good puppy," she said, but when she shut the door, Pumpkin yipped and whined and looked so sad. Emily sighed. There was nothing more she could do.

Covering her ears, she forced herself to walk away from

Pumpkin.

CHAPTER 23

Answered Prayers

Emily took the road home. At the mailbox, she took a deep breath and opened the door. Inside were two letters, but they weren't from her brother. Her chest tightened. Old worries returned. *Why wasn't he writing to them? Or was he, and the letters couldn't reach them?*

She hurried up the driveway and saw Mom in the garden. Emily joined her, plopped down and handed over the mail. She picked up a clump of dirt and tossed it aside.

"No letters from Greg."

"No news can be good news," Mom said. "We must have faith, Emily. Greg's okay."

"But how do you know?" Emily asked. She wanted proof.

"I trust it to be true. And you must, too."

Emily didn't think she could, but she nodded anyway.

"Help me pick beans," Mom said. She moved to a new row and Emily joined her. Their late planting of beans had flourished, and it took half an hour to pick through all the bushes.

Mom lifted the produce basket to her hip. "I'm glad that job's done. Let's make something yummy for dinner."

On the way to the house they talked about the menu and decided to have macaroni and cheese, tomato slices, cucumbers in vinegar and sugar, and zucchini bread for dessert. Mom got to work shredding zucchini while Emily cut cheese into chunks. For the next two hours, Emily was absorbed in the sounds and smells of the kitchen. As her hunger grew, her tummy growled.

Grandpa entered the kitchen. "What smells wonderful?" he asked.

"Zucchini bread," Emily said.

"Dinner will be ready soon," Mom said. "How are things with Winston?"

"His house is back in order," Dad said.

"We cleaned out Winston's screened porch," Grandpa said. "Pumpkin will stay there for now."

Emily frowned as she finished slicing cucumbers. "Pumpkin won't like it. She'd be happier in the kennel with her mother."

"That's true," Dad said. "But Mr. Brock wants her close by. Truthfully, I think he likes the pup. And, Clara, he's accepted your offer to cook for him while his leg heals."

Mom smiled. "Good. I've been hoping he would."

"Grandpa will still check in on him and feed the dogs," Dad continued, "and I'll round up some men to chop wood for him for the winter."

Grandpa put a hand on Emily's shoulder. "I'd like you to exercise his dogs every day. All of them."

"I will," she said.

Mom pulled the zucchini bread from the oven, then stopped and turned. "Did you hear that?"

"Am I in time for dinner?"

Mom dropped the pan.

"Greg!" Emily squealed. She reached him first and threw herself into his warm embrace. Her body shook, and tears flowed down her cheeks.

She felt Mom's arms around them, and Dad's, and then Grandpa's.

"Son," Dad whispered. "Welcome home."

They stayed that way for a while, glued together with love before untangling and wiping their eyes. And then Greg hugged each of them separately.

"It sure is great to be home," he said.

Mom touched his face and took his hands in hers. "I'm so happy you're here. We've been waiting for a letter, or phone call, telling us when you'd be coming home."

Greg leaned against the table. "I mailed a letter two weeks ago."

"We didn't get it," Emily said. "We got fourteen letters last week, but they were from August."

When he looked at her, Emily suddenly felt shy. Her brother seemed older, quieter. And he was thin in his wrinkled uniform. She thought Greg's eyes were filled with sadness, or maybe he was tired from traveling.

"It's a different life over there. And it's hard to send letters when we're out on missions."

"You should have called us, Son." Dad said. "We would have picked you up at the airport."

"That was the plan, but once I got stateside I changed my mind. If I had called, the whole town would have known through the party line. I need some time to adjust to being home."

"Whatever you need is fine with us," Dad said.

"Who brought you all the way to Freeland?" Grandpa asked.

"I caught a ride, but let's talk about that later," Greg said. "Right now, I'm starving!"

Mom set a place for Greg, and he asked lots of questions between forkfuls of food. He wanted to know about Uncle Tim and Aunt Chris and Sarah. He asked about some of his old high school friends, the status of the football team, and if the town had changed at all.

Then, during dessert, Greg sat back and clasped his hands together. "It's obvious something happened to Queenie. I've noticed nobody wrote about her."

"She was killed by a car," Dad said. "We couldn't tell you that in a letter."

Greg looked down at his hands. "When did it happen?

"The last day of school," Emily said as tears filled her eyes. "I called and called her, but she couldn't hear me. The car didn't stop, and then she was gone."

Greg slid next to her and took her hands in his. "Listen to me, Em. Queenie had trouble hearing before I enlisted. I guess I knew she had died, but I had to ask to be sure."

"Are you mad at me?" Emily asked.

"I'm sad, but not mad. I don't blame you. I don't blame anyone."

"But I was supposed to keep her safe, and I didn't. I'm really sorry."

"Accidents happen," Greg said. "It wasn't your fault."

For a while, everyone was quiet. Finally, Greg spoke. "Paul's missing in action. Did you know?"

Dad cleared his throat. "Yes. Mr. Brock received a telegram."

"At least he knows," Greg said. "I heard right before I left Nam. I'm having a really hard time with it."

"That's understandable," Grandpa said.

"Mr. Brock must be devastated. I'll go see him tomorrow. He has to know the military will do all they can to find Paul."

"He's counting on that," Dad said.

Greg stood and stretched. "If there is no other news to share right now, I'd like to take a walk around the property with Dad and Grandpa." He picked up Mom and easily swung her around. "Dinner was delicious. There's nothing like home cooking."

He then winked at Emily. "Save some time for me later on."

As the men left the house, Mom moved to the table and slid into a chair. Emily couldn't quite read her expression and was worried until her face lit up, and she said, "My son is home. He's really here!"

Emily felt the same way. Greg was home and it was wonderful and unbelievable at the same time.

"We need to have a welcome home party," Mom stated. "Just family. We'll keep it small. Greg will like that." She rushed around the kitchen, gathering up the dishes and putting them in the sink.

Emily watched her zoom about. *What was happening?*

Throwing the dish towel over her shoulder, Mom spun around. "I'll call Aunt Chris. I'll let Frannie know, but the restaurant is open tomorrow, so she probably won't be able to make it, but I bet Mr. Brock will come. That's it: Aunt Chris, Sarah, Frannie, Winston. And us!"

Emily didn't know what to say. She simply smiled, waiting for Mom to come back to earth.

Mom took a deep breath and held out her hand. "Will you help me with the menu?"

She took Mom's hand. "Of course. But shouldn't we check with Greg. Just to be sure he's okay with it?"

Mom nodded and touched Emily's cheek. "Absolutely. I should have thought of that."

***

Sitting outside on the kitchen steps, with a basket of green beans between them, Emily and Mom snipped beans and waited for the men to return from their walk. Emily spied them down by the orchard. They were laughing and patting each other on the back. It made her feel happy to see them happy.

Grandpa, Dad and Greg joined them, and for the next hour they worked together, snipping beans and chatting about Greg's growing up years and the pranks he and Paul pulled off. Emily laughed so hard she almost peed her pants. It felt good to laugh together as a family. She didn't want their good time to end.

But Greg kept looking across the field toward Mr. Brock's house. "I'm going to see him."

"I'll go with you, if you want, Son," Dad offered.

Greg shook his head. "I gotta do this on my own."

After he left everyone grew quiet. It was as if Greg took the air with him.

CHAPTER 24

The Unexpected

Emily woke with a smile, thinking what a great day it was going to be because had agreed to a small welcome home party. She threw off the covers and got dressed. She even made her bed and brushed her teeth before skipping down the stairs and into the kitchen.

Greg and Mom sat at the table drinking coffee. She overheard them talking about Jack-O and Beanie. Emily crossed the room and sat beside Greg. At the same time, Mom got up from the table in a hurry and tightened the belt on her robe. "We have so much to do for the welcome home party. Everyone will be here around two o'clock."

"But aren't we going to church?" Emily asked.

"Not today. I might fall to pieces if someone asks me about Greg, and I have to pretend he's not here."

Greg touched her arm gently. "Tomorrow you can tell the whole town, Mom. Today belongs to us."

Mom nodded and went upstairs. Emily had her brother all to herself.

"Let's take a walk, Sis. Will you show me where Queenie is buried?"

Emily took his hand and led the way to the apple orchard and Queenie's grave. Standing quietly together, she told him more about the day his dog died.

"When I got home from school, I rode my bike. Queenie chased me up and down the driveway, and then she went into the road. I called her, but she didn't come back. And then the car drove by, real fast, and hit her." Emily squeezed her eyes shut at the memory. Her breath caught in her throat.

Greg put an arm around her. "There was nothing you could have done."

Emily didn't answer.

"Queenie died because she was in the road at the wrong time."

"I miss her lots," Emily said. "Knight died, too."

Greg sighed. "Mr. Brock told me. So, let's do something to honor him. Let's put rocks on Knight's grave, like you did here for Queenie. We can do it together, just you and me."

"Sure," Emily said. "I have lots more rocks."

"Is there anything else you want to talk about, like Pumpkin?"

"Well, I miss her so much. But I can't have her and that's that."

"Are you sure?" Greg asked. "Did you try everything, with all your heart, to persuade Mr. Brock to give her to you?"

Emily nodded. "I did. I said I'd buy her, and that I'd take care of her. And that I love her. But Mr. Brock wants to keep her for Paul."

"That's all I wanted to know. If you tried your very best, fought the very best fight to get Pumpkin, then you have done all you could."

Emily considered his words, which made her remember back to when Sarah had told her to fight for Pumpkin. *Had she really done all she could?* Her mind began to spin.

"Let's go home," Greg said. "I'd like to help with the party preparations."

As they walked into the yard, Grandpa pulled up to the

house. His truck was filled with groceries. Greg unloaded the bags and boxes and Emily sorted everything into piles. After that, she sliced cabbage for coleslaw and Mom finished cutting up the eggs for potato salad.

Time slipped by and aromas filled the kitchen. Around noon, Emily peered out the window. Dad and Greg were setting up the card table and chairs, and Grandpa was up to his elbows in soapy water scrubbing their homemade grill. But all she could think about was Pumpkin. *Was there something more she could do?*

"Look at the time," Mom said. "Our guests will be here in one hour." She handed Emily a stack of dishes. "Take these to the picnic table, dear, and please ask your brother to come see me."

Emily ran outside. She almost collided with Greg.

"What's the rush?" he asked.

"Mom needs you," she said, "and I've got something important I have to do. I'll be back as quick as I can."

"Okay," Greg said with a smile. "But don't be late for my party."

Emily ran upstairs and grabbed her piggy bank. Then she jumped on her bike and peddled hard down the driveway.

Pumpkin, I'm coming. I'm going to fight for you with everything I have.

She turned into Mr. Brock's driveway, sailed up to the porch and laid on the brakes. Thank goodness his truck was there.

"Mr. Brock? Mr. Brock?" Emily jumped off the bike and ran up the steps. "Mr. Brock? I've come to talk about Pumpkin."

The screened door opened, and a small bundle of energy bolted out. The furry critter stood on her hindlegs and danced for Emily.

"Pumpkin!" She lifted the pup and received a dozen sloppy licks.

Leaning on his cane, Mr. Brock slowly made his way outside. "What's all the ruckus about?"

"Mr. Brock, I want Pumpkin. I need Pumpkin. I can't stop thinking about her. Every day, all day, she's all I want." She held out her piggy bank. "I'll give you all the money I have. I want to buy Pumpkin."

"I don't want your money," Mr. Brock said.

"You still have Lilyanne, Sir Taylor, and Dandy Lady. You don't need Pumpkin. I do. I need her."

Mr. Brock scratched his chin. "She's high-spirited. What makes you so sure you can handle her?"

"Because we are meant for each other."

Pumpkin squirmed in her arms, so Emily put her down. The pup ran to Emily's bike and sat beside it.

With the help of his cane, Mr. Brock took a few steps down his porch, then lowered himself into a rocking chair.

"I've been thinking a lot about Paul. What he would want me to do."

Emily held her breath. *He'd tell you to give her to me.*

"You took good care of my dogs these past weeks," Mr. Brock said. "I'm thankful for that…for all you and your grandpa did."

Emily waited, still holding out the piggy bank.

"I guess I could get another dog when Paul comes home. If he wants one."

Emily's heart thumped. She waited to hear more.

"If she causes any trouble, though, you can't bring her back."

"Wait. You're giving me Pumpkin?" She paused. "For sure?"

Mr. Brock nodded.

"I won't ever bring her back," Emily promised. "Thank you, Mr. Brock. Thank you." She saw a hint of a smile on his face.

"Put your bike in the truck bed," he said. "I'll take you home since I'm on my way to Greg's party."

They didn't talk at all while driving back to her house, but that was okay with Emily. She'd pretty much used up all her words fighting for Pumpkin.

They parked by the house and Emily climbed out. She took Pumpkin from the truck seat and placed her on the ground. Pumpkin went wild, running in circles, barking and rolling in the grass.

"What's going on here," Dad said as he and Grandpa walked over. Grandpa helped Winston out of the truck.

"Your girl fought hard, and wore me down," Mr. Brock said. "The pup is hers, and there will be no more discussion on it."

Emily grinned from ear to ear. "I hope you're not mad, Dad. I know you didn't want a dog."

"But you did, and that's all that matters," he replied.

"Ahem." Greg nudged Emily's shoulder. "Are you going

to properly introduce us?"

Emily giggled and handed over the pup. "This is Pumpkin. Pumpkin, this is my brother."

Pumpkin cocked her head and barked in his face.

Greg laughed. "She's bold, and loud."

"She can be our dog," Emily told him. "We'll train her together."

"No way." Greg shook his head. "She belongs to you and you alone. Say it out loud. You need to believe it."

Emily searched her brother's face, and saw he meant it. "Pumpkin is my dog!"

"Glad that's settled." Greg handed the pup back.

Aunt Chris and Sarah arrived shortly thereafter. Emily ran to the car to show off Pumpkin.

"Look who I have," Emily said.

"Wait a minute," Sarah said. "Does she still belong to Mr. Brock?"

"Nope. I fought for her one more time, and it worked!"

"Good golly!" Sarah's face lit up. "You finally have Pumpkin!"

Mom and Aunt Chris served iced tea and lemonade, and Dad put hamburger patties on the grill. The men sat in the shade, asking Greg questions about Vietnam, troop morale, and other stuff while Emily and the others listened. After that, the girls played in the yard with Pumpkin.

Emily thought it was the most perfect day.

"Ken?" Mom sniffed the air. "Is something burning?"

"Oh, no!" Dad dashed to the grill. "Everyone like charred burgers?"

As everyone filled their plates, Emily slid into a chair. She rubbed Pumpkin's silky ears. She still found it hard to believe the pup was hers, for now and always. And then she remembered something Mom had told her. Some problems need extra time to work themselves out. This one sure did.

She snuggled Pumpkin and whispered, "I'm never going to let you go."

But Pumpkin, unable to contain herself, wriggled from her arms and headed straight for the food table.

THE END

Acknowledgements:

To create this book, many hours were spent in lots of chairs with either pen in hand or staring at/typing on a computer. Many hours . . . many. This story began a long, long time ago in a land called Beaverton where Craig and I raised our girls, and where I would grasp precious time and sequester myself in my little writing nook. Back then, I thought I knew how to write. I quickly realized how much I didn't know. So, the publishing of this book is truly a dream come true.

I thank God for giving me the gift of writing. I've been able to use it throughout my life in both business and personal matters. I thank my hubby, Craig, and our girls, Lindsay and Tanya, for believing in me and saying they loved my writing even in my early learning days. My extended family members have been very supportive over the years, many of them reading fledgling manuscripts.

Thanks to my sister, Sandy Rae, for reading the "almost" final copy and for offering excellent editing comments. And there are some critique partners I need to mention: Linda Egeler, Erin Fanning, and Janice Broyles; these gals encouraged me to keep on telling Emily's story - thank you (BIG HUGS). To everyone else who read chapters and offered valuable critiques - thank you as well.

I must give special credit to three veterans who answered my questions based upon their service in the Vietnam War - Tom Winchell, Rod Sparks, and Marc Leepson. Their recollections greatly enhanced this story, and I'm so thankful for their assistance.

To wrap this up, my heartfelt thanks to editor and friend, Janice Broyles, of Late November Literary, for insisting The Puppy Predicament must be published. I am honored.

9 781734 100860